BALLS & CHAIN

Praise for *The Jesus Injection*

"Fast paced and readable, Eric Andrew-Katz's *The Jesus Injection* is a character-driven mystery with familiar political scenery and a well put together paranoic's nightmare of a credible story line."—Felice Picano, author of *Like People In History*

"A hilariously irreverent satire."—John Rechy, author of *City of Night*

"Meet the hero for the new century...Agent Buck 98!"—*The Jesus Injection*—And if that title sounds strange and intriguing, you don't even know the half of it!! The unstoppable undercover duo—Agent Buck 98 and his partner, Noxia Von Tussell—do fabulously gay battle against bigots, mad scientists, politicians, and deceptively handsome hit men to SAVE HUMANITY!!! And still find time for romance, fashion, smart-ass remarks, and the occasional well-deserved cocktail."—*New York Times* best-selling author Alison Arngrim

"And there is lots of action. Andrews-Katz certainly knows his way around a fight scene, and the climax is nicely terse and well done."—*Out in Print*

"Andrews-Katz displays a keen ear for dialogue and a good sense of style and humor. I look forward to more from him."
—*Seattle Gay News*

By the Author

The Jesus Injection

Balls & Chain

BALLS & CHAIN

by

Eric Andrews-Katz

A Division of Bold Strokes Books

2014

ISBN 13: 978-1-62639-218-2

This Trade Paperback Original Is Published By
Bold Strokes Books, Inc.
P.O. Box 249
Valley Falls, NY 12185

First Edition: November 2014

CREDITS
EDITORS: GREG HERREN AND STACIA SEAMAN
PRODUCTION DESIGN: STACIA SEAMAN
COVER DESIGN BY SHERI (GRAPHICARTIST2020@HOTMAIL.COM)

Acknowledgments

The second time the journey from story idea to publication occurs is no less difficult or frightening than the first. Again, I'm very fortunate to have not traveled it alone and am extremely grateful to those who have helped me along in finding my way.

To Len Barot of Bold Strokes Books—thank you for seeing Buck's potential and believing in me enough to share him with so many others. Also to Greg Herren for his patience and guidance along the editing pathway. An extended thank you must go to the friends formed at the Saints and Sinners Festival, and especially to the Bold Strokes Books family for their united support and energy. There are several people who push from the realms of cyber worlds, and their kick-start inspirations are much appreciated: Barbara, Connie, Jove, Melissa, Sheri, Victoria, Yvonne, and the many others who continuously encourage—thank you for your blitzing.

Felice—you are an inspiration and I appreciate the many, many doors you've opened for me.

Jameson—thank you for the opportunities you consistently throw my way.

It's an extremely rare day that I don't want to go into my massage office, and a good percentage of the reason is the friends and clientele that I see on a (semi) regular basis. Some like to be quiet and allow me time in my head. Others are chatty, and some interact on such a level that it's a question as to which of us gets more therapy. For these reasons and more, I'd like to express great thanks to: Brad, David, Ed, James, Jaimie, Lloyd, Mitch, Sally, Shaun, and especially Vincent.

To Brian for his help with political situations and terminology.

To Jake for his help on all situations dealing with sports.

To Stephen Cole (one of the moderators of the Forgotten Musicals site), thanks for the inspiration I didn't know I was looking for, and thank you to Rebecca DeVries McConnell and Nathan Cox for their help in answering musical theater questions on that Facebook page.

My friends are my family, and there are a few who go above and beyond quite frequently. Susan puts up with an endless amount of my teasing about children, but I am in awe of her. She manages to find a balance between her life activities, her mothering responsibilities, proofreading and giving feedback on my writing, and (seemingly) keeping a sense of humor all at the same time. Irene, I don't say enough how much I appreciate you—I do. Greg, I admire that you are never short of an opinion and grateful that you are usually using it in my favor. Byron—I'm thankful for your input in my life.

Debbie—I met you once on a plane, but you continue to inspire me with your resilience.

Alison—You are amazing with your unending dedication to many different causes. Thank you from a grateful community!

Jama—Thank you for being a light when I find myself in darkness. Thank you for being a voice of reason among shouts of insanity. You do me great honors by being my friend, and I am a better man for it.

For my husband Alan. Words cannot express how much you mean to me. You can make Pollyanna seem demonic and the reverse (although I am usually the only one to see it), and somehow you continue to put up with me no matter what I do. Nothing in this world has any right being perfect. I'm grateful that—for me at least—you are as close as you are.

There are many more people I have accidentally omitted, although their support has been present, and I am very grateful to them.

To Alan,
The proof soul mates exist

CHAPTER ONE

The smack from behind made Buck jolt forward from his aisle seat on the plane. He took out one of his ear buds so he could turn around and, once again, reprimand the five-year-old kicking the seat from behind.

"Sorry," he heard in the heavily accented voice of the actual culprit.

Buck looked up to see the black jacket and pants of the Hasidic man carefully making his way to the front of the plane. The middle-aged man with the shaggy beard and side curls hanging past his ears offered a brief apologetic smile before continuing one step at a time, using the headrest of each seat to steady his step. It was his third trip up and down the aisles.

"I wonder if it's exercise or a small bladder," Buck muttered. Settling back into his chair, he replaced the ear bud and let the sweet serenity of Audra McDonald's soprano voice calm his nerves and, with the help of the steady, low purr of the engines, lull him back into relaxation. As Audra began to lament the man that got away, another jolt from behind disrupted Buck's leisure. Undeniably this time it came from the child.

Agent Buck 98 opened his hazel eyes, then narrowed them to angry slits. Clenching his jaw, but not too tightly to avoid damage to his perfect smile, he curled around the seat edge to stare down the child.

"Kick me again," Buck started with a low growl, "and Santa won't be bringing you nothin'."

The boy's face melted and his bottom lip quivered.

"That's awful," the mother sitting next to the child reprimanded Buck. "He's just a child. It takes a village, you know."

"Wrong," Buck corrected her. "It *should* only take one responsible adult. Please let me know when you find one."

"Ladies and gentleman. May I please have your attention." The heavily Germanic-accented voice crackled through the plane's PA system.

Buck turned around and saw the Hasidic man at the front of the plane, standing between the first class and coach dividing curtains.

The man couldn't have stood more than five foot seven, with the slightly rounded shoulders of age bringing him down an inch. The fringes of the prayer shawl hung out the bottom of his jacket and the long-sleeved, pressed white shirt showed from underneath. He held his hands in the air and lowered them to quiet the people on the plane, as if he were about to tell a bedtime story to his grandchildren.

"Sir," said a blond male attendant wearing the airline's uniform and approaching from the front of first class. He spoke to the man as if talking to a challenged child, holding his hand out for the speaker. "This is for emergency use *only*. Please sit down and stop playing around."

The elderly man looked at the attendant for a moment before capitulating and offering the microphone with a shaky hand. The device slipped, letting the elastic cord pull it into the wall with a thud. The attendant let out an audible exasperated sigh and bent down to pull on the spiral cord to retrieve the microphone.

In a flash the older man grabbed him with a firm grasp. He pushed him downward and brought his black-clothed knee up to collide with the younger man's chin. The attendant flew backward and crashed into the bathroom door. The accordion closure opened and the attendant slid to the floor.

The terrorist picked up the speaker and stood with his back to the bathroom door.

"Anyone else want to be a hero?" The harsh voice was suddenly free of any type of accent. All traces of old age or feebleness instantly vanished.

He now stood fully erect, taller than before and more menacing. All traces of frailty were cast aside. Blue eyes blazed out from bushy eyebrows grown over like a dormant caterpillar. The ringlets of hair shook with rage as they fell from under the old-world, wide-brimmed hat. Dulled, uneven teeth shone out from a dark mustache and shaggy beard.

"I have smeared a highly flammable paste onto all of your headrests. I have dragged it along my feet, spreading it on the aisle carpets."

The man reached into his jacket pocket and took out a cell phone. He held it up for all to see, turning his head back and forth between first class and coach as if watching a high-speed tennis match.

"If I press two digits, the phone explodes and ignites the front rows immediately. How's that for priority seating?"

A few cries and frightened murmurs flooded the front rows. The man reached over and pressed one button with an overly exaggerated gesture. He held the phone into the microphone to let the audible beep echo throughout the plane.

"That was the first, and believe me, I can press another faster than any of you can reach me. So no one try to be a hero. You six in first class," he gestured with his chin, "get back here, you elitist pigs!"

The microphone fell from his hand and crashed into the wall, causing the front row of coach to jump in their buckled seats. The passengers up front unbuckled their belts slowly, standing in the aisle as best they could. Reaching into his other pocket, the man took out a small tube of toothpaste and, using his teeth, removed the cap. With his free hand he expelled the paste into his palm.

"Move! Move! Get to the back of the plane. Now!" the rabid rabbi snarled. He slapped his palm against the back of each passenger rushing past, spreading the flammable paste onto their clothes and neck. The six passengers herded to the aircraft's back rows. Once the first class cabin was cleared, he stepped back to address everyone in coach.

"This plane has been taken over in the name of the Orthodox Zionist Nation. We are tired of interference with our homeland from Palestine and their sympathizers! I want to see a pilot appear with his hands behind his head, or this plane will make the *Hindenburg* seem like a matchstick! The rest of you stay buckled in your seats!"

The wild blue eyes blazed red with rage. White spittle formed at the corner of his bearded lips, randomly spraying forth with each rant.

Agent 98 watched carefully from his aisle seat in the fourth row. His mind raced to calculate the distance between his seat and the front, and how fast at best and at worst the rabbi could press a keyboard digit. His hand crept down, touching the metal buckle, readying to spring it open.

A sudden kick from behind caused his hand to slip, cutting the side of his palm on the edge of the metal. Gritting his teeth, he locked his eyes on the terrorist up front.

"Will you keep that damn brat still," Buck hissed back between his seat and the lady sitting against the window.

"He's a child." The woman behind leaned forward. "He's frightened. You don't need to add to it."

"Really, lady?" Buck said incredulously. "Are you kidding me with that?"

The pilot appeared, causing the cabin to go silent. He was a man of average build, dressed in a blue uniform with his hands placed behind his head. Brown hair brushed forward capped a low forehead and rounded face. He slowly approached the man dressed in black.

"I'm the copilot, Captain Dyson," the man said as he got closer. Each step was slow and deliberate, to show he meant no harm. "We don't want anyone to get hurt. What can we do to help you?"

The terrorist's chest rose and fell with each sharp breath. Every movement he made was a jerky twitch.

"You're taking the plane to Zacatecas, Mexico," he barked out. "We will completely refuel in fifteen minutes or less, or I'll blow up the plane. If you can do that, I'll let four passengers go— of my choosing. No one is allowed on or off until that moment."

"I can't do that," Captain Dyson calmly replied.

The passengers on the plane erupted in protest. Shouts of anger, fear, and frustration rang throughout the cabin.

"Shut up!" the terrorist screamed into the microphone. The plane immediately went silent except for the hum of the engines. "You will do exactly what I say or I'll blow the plane up now, and we all fall thirty thousand feet."

"Look," Captain Dyson said firmly, "I can't do that."

The terrorist nodded in understanding. He thought a moment, glancing over the passengers. Without warning he sprang forward, ramming his fist into the underside of the captain's chin. The blow sent Dyson reeling and he fell beyond the sheer curtain. His head hit the armrest of a first class chair, and he rolled facedown into the aisle.

Moving with agility beyond his appearance, the terrorist leapt onto the pilot's back. Reaching down he took hold of the captain's head and gave it a firm twist. An audible "crack" was heard over the lull of the jet's humming. The body dropped, the face hitting the carpeted floor. The head lay at an odd angle.

In a flash the terrorist stood and turned around, standing over the body like a lion with its kill. His chest rose and fell quickly. The wildly rounded blue eyes stared at the passengers, all too stunned to move, stilled with fear and remaining buckled in their seats.

"Any other heroes?" the terrorist cried out. No one answered. The man stepped back into the cabin and reached for the microphone dangling against the wall.

"I want these television screens to show our route! If we aren't heading toward Mexico, I'll blow up this entire flight."

The cell phone was raised high above his head. His chest slowed as his breath regulated. All eyes locked onto the video screens randomly set throughout the cabin. Only the sounds of engines burning through the sky filled the plane.

Another moment crawled by. The man raised his second hand above his head and pointed his index finger at the phone. His lips moved with silent prayers.

The television screens simultaneously blinked into snowstorms. A picture emerged showing a clear outline of the West Coast of the United States. The digital image of the plane veered off the path across the country and headed south toward California.

"The captain should never have admitted they couldn't meet the terrorist's demands." Agent Buck 98 couldn't help himself from critiquing the actions of others. "That was his first mistake."

Tension prowled the plane's aisles. The woman in the window seat next to Buck sat rigid with her eyes closed, busily working her rosary necklace between her fingers. Buck took a deep breath, determined not to get sucked into the undertow of panic, and analyzed the situation.

His right hand crept into his jacket pocket and easily withdrew a thick ballpoint pen. Using his thumb he clicked the end several times in succession, carefully counting each one. The inner chamber turned with each click, allowing access to a different-colored ink tube.

"Three," Buck counted and clicked. "Four and—"

The sudden jolt from behind made him drop the pen into his lap.

"Listen." Buck pressed his cheek against the seat back cushion, hissing between the seats. "If you don't keep that damn kid still, you're going to get us all killed!"

"He's frightened," the mother argued. "What do you expect from a child?"

"Keep him still," Buck snapped back, "or the last thing I do before I die is rip his leg off and beat him senseless!"

Agent 98 turned back to the situation at hand. The terrorist was fixated on the video screen, occasionally glancing across the cabin at the fearful passengers.

Buck picked up the ballpoint pen and gave it a quick study.

"I was on four," he recalled and clicked one final time.

Agent 98's fingers nimbly unscrewed the pen, removing the inner spring. The pen's body was divided into five separate tubes. Four held color cartridges, while the last one remained sealed at the end with the letter "X." He broke off the metal pocket clip, puncturing the tube, and replaced the cap.

Holding the pen away from his body, he clicked the end. Several droplets ran off the ballpoint's tip, falling onto the carpet.

"Maybe when I'm done," Buck said, a malicious smile crossing his lips, "I'll accidentally shoot the kid behind me."

Agent 98 clutched the pen tightly in his fist. Slowly, he brought his hand to his lips as if covering a yawn. He drew in a large breath, holding it as long as possible before fully exhaling, building his lungs' power. With another breath he touched the edge of the pen to his lips. Counting mentally, Buck waited for his chance to act.

The terrorist leaned against the wall. He studied the passengers being held hostage. All those terrified, panicked eyes stared back at him.

The window of opportunity was minimal and Agent 98 knew there was no second chance. The timing was crucial. His mark was clear and his only shot presented itself. Buck took a final deep breath. He opened his mouth and felt the edge of the pen touch his lips. Wrapping his tongue around the shaft to hold it steady, Agent 98 aimed for the small bit of exposed flesh of the neck, counted to three, and blew out as hard as he could.

The sudden kick from behind jolted the edge of Buck's elbow, sending the dart off its mark. Missing the terrorist's neck, the needle hit the collar of the white shirt. A red flower blossomed onto the cloth and bled out underneath the jacket.

The man's head snapped to study the spreading crimson. His face grew darker and constricted with fury. He looked at the passengers, his chest rising and falling with rage.

"In drerd arayn!" the terrorist cried out. He held up the cell phone, showing it to the terrified passengers, who watched helplessly. "See you all in hell!"

The plane erupted in screams as the terrorist pressed the remaining digit.

CHAPTER TWO

The red light exploded inside the airplane's cabin as soon as the cell phone's digit was pressed. A shrill alarm rang out, filling the interior, causing the passengers to cover their ears. Ten seconds later it stopped. The plane flooded with white lights. People immediately transitioned from panic to calm chatter, unbuckling their seat belts, standing and stretching in the aisles. The side of the plane slid apart as if it were the doors of an elevator and people calmly moved out into the insulated plane hangar's simulation training area.

"Agent 98!" said a paternal-sounding voice.

Buck froze in place when he heard his name and rank. Standing on the edge of the studio's set, he dropped his head, realizing he was not going to escape unnoticed and avoid the anticipated reprimand. Taking a deep breath and raising his head, Buck ran a hand through his chestnut hair. Turning to the approaching man dressed in a fastidious black suit, he succumbed to the inevitable.

"Thank you for flying with our airlines," Buck said with an overly charming smile and exaggerated kindness. "Buh-bye now. Please fly with us again, buh-bye."

Agent 69 approached with his hands clasped behind his back, his favorite patronizing position. At five foot eleven he stood slightly over Buck, but the pear shape of his body and the balding likeness to Alfred Hitchcock made him more of an imposing figure.

"Nice choice of armament," Agent 69 said. He rocked back onto his heels, clapping his hand into his palm behind his back. "Bad execution."

"I would have done better if it weren't so god-awful early in the morning," Agent 98 said. He forced a yawn that sounded too loud and stretched to his arms' limit above his head. "You know, the last time I saw six thirty a.m., it was from the other side. I was going to bed. Not doing a work exercise."

"Boo hoo," was Agent 69's reply. "Cry me a river."

"You know I would have brought down that terrorist in a minute," Buck said defensively. He spotted the child walking out of the plane and took an aggressive step toward him, causing the kid to scamper away. "But that damn kid kept on kicking the back of my chair."

"And you can never know what obstacles you may encounter," Agent 69 said. He walked off the set with Buck close behind. "That's the point of these exercises. A good agent can handle anything."

Agent 69 led Buck across the room and away from the actors congregating at the food table.

"A good parent controls their child in public!" Buck muttered. "You know my aim is better than that. That kid threw me off my game."

"Get over it, Agent 98," the Hitchcock doppelganger said with a heavy sigh. "I'm sure this isn't the first time you botched a blow job."

"Muffin!" Buck snapped back. "Getting humorous in your old age? In another ten years you might even be funny!"

"So I've been told. And when will you stop calling me Muffin?"

"When you change your agent number from 69," Buck answered nonchalantly. He took a large step, putting him at Muffin's side. "It just doesn't feel right on my tongue."

Agent 69 rolled his eyes. The two men stopped midway against one of the side walls of the hangar. A small dark bulb was inserted centrally above the outline of a doorway. Immediately to the right were three small triangles shaped in a hazmat circle above an empty screen the size of a paperback book.

"The blowgun pen was my own personal invention," Muffin said, placing his hand on the screen. A light flashed across his palm and the dark bulb pulsed emerald green. "With your hot air I'm sure you could propel a dart hard enough to bring down an elephant."

"That's hi-larious, Muffin," Buck said snidely. "I'm thinking of smacking down an ass right now."

"Leave your private life at home, Agent 98."

From inside the wall a motor started to hum softly. Using his free hand, Agent 69 pushed the triangular buttons in a memorized sequence. After more mechanisms sounded the door slid open.

"Out of curiosity and personal vanity," Agent 69 said, gesturing for Buck to enter first, "what made you choose that particular weapon?"

"It's the only one that made sense," Buck answered. He gave his fellow agent an incredulous look. "Guns and liquids would all be detected and confiscated at security. Any kind of blade, even those hidden in the cleverest of devices, would still be seen on an x-ray. This one would show every indication of being a normal pen. If tested, the ink would write anything desired. It's elementary, my dear Muffin."

Buck flashed a tight-lipped smile and walked ahead.

The men entered a room with a long table in the middle, surrounded by six empty chairs. Atop the table were three different brightly colored folders: green, orange, and blue. A set of glasses surrounded a large pitcher filled with ice water. Buck took a seat and poured himself a drink.

"Inside the folders you will find your next assignment," Agent 69 said, pointing to the tabletop.

Buck opened the top orange folder to see the photo of a

handsome man smiling back. The gentleman was obviously Latino from the brown skin and dark wavy hair curling up and away from his forehead. Brown eyes sparkled happily and a black goatee and mustache covered a Mona Lisa half-smile, making the viewer wonder what the subject was thinking. His shoulders appeared broad through the suit jacket he wore, and behind him the Florida state flag hung with the American flag next to it.

"Do you know who that is?" Agent 69 asked.

"Judging from the two flags, I'm guessing Ponce de León?"

"That is incorrect," Muffin chided. "That is Miguel Reyes, the openly gay governor of Florida, seeking out his second term."

"Oh yeah," Buck exclaimed, taking a second look at the photo. "Is he the first openly gay governor of any Southern state?"

"I'm not sure," Muffin answered. "But he's one of the few, if not. He's responsible for Referendum 65, the initiative to make marriage equality legal throughout the state of Florida. He would *definitely* be the first Southern official to do that."

"It's about time," Buck said snidely. "The South always seems to be about a decade behind the rest of the country when it comes to civil rights."

"Do tell me how you really feel."

"Well, it seems there are more pedophiles in the South," Buck rambled on without sensing the sarcasm. "At least if you watch the predator sting shows. Then there is the large percentage of child crimes including murder that just seem to happen more in the South than any other area of the country."

"Are you quite done now?" Agent 69 asked. His tone immediately invoked silence. "Alejandro, the governor's son, was kidnapped this morning at approximately eight thirty Eastern time."

"You sure it was a kidnapping?" Buck said with a sneer. "Kids run off all the time. More than likely it was the mother not wanting her kid to be raised by a gay guy."

"Not the case," Agent 69 said. "There is no mother in this

situation. Governor Reyes is a single parent. Then there's the note that was left."

"Why didn't you say so?"

"Why didn't you give me the chance?"

"You are so cute when you're being smug." Buck blew a kiss that crashed against Agent 69's stoic expression. He immediately sat up and became more serious. "Continue."

"Governor Reyes was elected only after two recounts due to the closeness of the race," Muffin explained. "But because of the good work he's done, his popularity has increased. It was then that he helped write R-65 and is trying to get it passed through the state's legislature."

"In the South? That's ambitious. I applaud him and his," Buck used his fingers for air quotes, "'special friend.' I'm sure that's how they are still referred to down there."

"Governor Reyes is currently single."

"You now have my complete attention." Buck reexamined the photo.

Agent 69 gave a heavy sigh. "Will you please pay attention to the issue at hand? Marriage should be for everyone, don't you agree?"

"Actually, Muffin…" Buck leaned back in his chair. His fingers spun the glass on the table. "I don't know if I like the term 'marriage' for gay relationships. I'm not sure gay men and women mimicking heterosexual relationships is the proper way to go."

"And somewhere," Muffin muttered, "Larry Kramer is weeping."

"Let me finish!" Buck insisted. "Just because I don't foresee myself going down the path of matrimony doesn't mean I don't think others should have the same legal rights. I just think we can come up with some alternative name that gives the same meaning. What's it that heterosexual hypocrites like to say? 'I think gay people should get married…they should suffer along

ERIC ANDREWS-KATZ

with the rest of us!' It says a lot for the lifestyle we're trying to imitate."

"I think that's supposed to be a joke."

"You're telling me!" Buck crossed his legs and shut the folder.

"What would you suggest? Commitment ceremony? Soul mating? Handfasting? I can't wait to hear it."

"That's not my job," Buck said.

"No. Your job is going to take you to Florida." Buck opened his mouth to protest, but Agent 69 barreled on. "Your tickets, papers, and ID have all been set up and are included in the blue folder. As the saying goes, wheels up in thirty minutes, so if you're not going to listen to the assignment, you can figure it out on your own. I suggest you go home and pack up."

"Please tell me it's a direct flight to Tallahassee?" Buck said hesitantly.

"You know the state capital but you don't recognize the governor?"

"Some things just get ingrained from school," Buck explained with a shrug.

"Well, then not exactly. We'll be taking a private plane from here to Jacksonville. It should take us less than four hours. Since we don't want to bring any attention to the governor, you will be deplaning in Jacksonville to make a connection to Tallahassee. I'll be flying on directly. Your smaller commercial flight should put you at the governor's house by 1630 hours. I'll have more information for you by the time you land."

"What size are you talking about when you say 'smaller commercial flight'?" Buck stuttered.

"About the size of the simulation you just failed to prevent from exploding."

"Nice roundabout, Muffin," Buck said, nodding. "Isn't there anyone else who can do this assignment? What about Noxia? Can't she do it?"

• 14 •

"Why must you call her by that ridiculous name?" Agent 69 said with exasperation.

"Well, *Muffin!*" Buck said, emphasizing his point. "It's not ridiculous, it's German. And I only *gave* it to her. She chose to continue using it."

"You do like your nicknames, don't you?" Agent 69 muttered with a shake of his head. "And I'll never understand why. Either way, no! She can't do this assignment. Besides, if your memory serves correctly..."

"And it does!" Out of habit Buck inserted the automatic response he and Noxia shared.

"She's taking her annual vacation. She always does for August and September."

"Oh yeah," Buck said. His head bobbed and his smile maliciously widened. Once again he used finger quotes. "Her yearly 'vacation.' Call it what it is, Muffin. Nip. Tuck. Clip. Suck."

"Why in the world would Agent 46 need any of that?" Agent 69 asked incredulously. "She's in almost perfect condition as an agent. Better than some others I could mention."

Buck's hand immediately went to his flat stomach, feeling his abdominals tighten.

"*Almost* perfect condition," he emphasized. "Every year she comes back from her holiday looking tanned and refreshed. Her hair is perfectly done with not a colored root out of place. Admit it. She's having work done. I wonder what it will be." Buck reached up to the sides of his eyes, pulling back the skin.

"Do you mind?" Agent 69 said, using his stricter paternal tone. "Stop being so distracting, I'm trying to fill you in on the details!"

Buck sat forward in his chair, leaning his elbows on the table. "Is all the information I need in one of these folders?"

"Yes," Muffin hesitantly admitted. "But there are other things you should know."

"Okay," Buck replied in a singsong manner. "What?"

"The local police cannot be notified," Agent 69 explained. "If the kidnappers think any authorities are involved, they will kill Alejandro."

"How old is this kid anyway?"

"He's fourteen," Muffin said. "So respect your maturity elders."

"Nice."

"You have one week to get this done, Agent 98!"

Muffin's tone commanded Buck's attention. It wasn't one he used often, but when he did, everyone who heard it, listened.

"I'm going to tell you this once." Agent 69 spoke softly, a calm chill in his voice like the eye of a hurricane. His words were spoken slowly to make sure each of them was precisely understood. "This is a very important mission. Whether or not anyone else is available is irrelevant. You were specifically chosen for this mission. I doubt there's anyone else who could get this particular job done under these circumstances."

"What are these circumstances?" Buck asked.

"You don't need to know that now. This mission is assigned to you, and *that* is all you need to know. So please, do me a favor: Pull your head out of your butt, get over that bias against children, and get ready to go to Florida!"

Buck sat still, feeling the verbal reprimand as if he'd just received a spanking. He gathered the folders together in silence, purposely avoiding eye contact with Agent 69.

"Do I pick up a car when I get to the airport?" Buck asked after a long silence.

"No," Agent 69 replied sharply. "I have a few modifications I need to arrange before we have a car ready for you."

Buck's face lit up with childish glee. "I always like when you have something new and fun for me. What's it going to be?"

"You'll just have to wait and find out," Muffin said. "There will be someone to pick you up at the airport in Tallahassee. I'll text you more information while you are en route. We'll meet up later."

The silence returned, making itself comfortable. Muffin gathered his papers and waited at the door for Agent 98. Taking his time, Buck slowly approached.

"The blowgun pen really is an ingenious idea," he muttered, casting his eyes downward and dragging his feet.

"I know." A heavy sigh accompanied the agent's reply. "I didn't get this job on my good looks and cheery disposition."

Muffin offered an out-of-character smile. Buck met his smile and raised it a humorous snort. He patted Muffin on the shoulder and went through the door he held open. They entered the plane hangar with the simulation exercise still on break. The passengers milled around talking amongst themselves, eating and drinking from the food tables scattered to the right.

"Who are these people anyway?" Buck asked.

"Local actors hired for the day," Muffin explained. "They are given a script and told to improvise accordingly. They think it's training for the airline industry."

"Each agent has a different script?" Buck asked inquisitively. He studied Muffin with a newly found admiration.

"Every agent is given the same arsenal choices as you were, and told they are going to have to get it through airport security. A random passenger is chosen in advance to take over and the agent's ability tested. No two simulations are the same, so no two agents take the same simulation."

"How did Noxia do on the exercise?" Buck asked with the interest of an impudent sibling. "I bet she failed, didn't she? Didn't she?"

"I'm beginning to figure out why you don't like children," Muffin said. "I'm guessing too much competition."

"Come on!" Buck said, ignoring the comment. "How'd she do? You can tell me."

"No. I cannot. I am prohibited from discussing other people's exams and scores, but the simple truth is that she hasn't taken it yet." Muffin walked over to a table to get a small pastry.

Buck studied the pear-shaped man with a doubting look. He looked over the people milling about in costume when a short alarm rang out. They all started making their way back and Buck saw the child from his failed exercise cutting past in front of him.

Reaching into his pocket, Buck withdrew the pen. His finger clicked the end several times.

"Agent 98?" Muffin warned as he approached. "What are you doing?"

"Getting a little revenge," Buck hissed. He took a deep breath, bringing the pen to his lips and taking careful aim.

"Don't do it!"

Muffin's warning came too late. Buck blew the dart and hit his mark on the back of the little boy's head. The child instinctively reached around at the brief stabbing and felt liquid on his fingers. He stopped. Looking at his hand, he saw the bright red of the colored water. Mistaking it for blood, the child let out a wailing scream.

"Now," Buck said, turning to Muffin with a final nod. "Now I'm ready to go."

CHAPTER THREE

The plane touched down as the child sitting next to Buck finally drifted off to sleep. As the aircraft came to a halt on the runway, the mother held the toddler against her chest, trying not to awaken the kraken.

"I'm going to let her sleep as long as I can," the mother explained to Buck. "This way she might stay asleep on the drive home."

"She should," Buck said. "She kept everyone else awake on the flight out here."

"Babies can be a handful," the mother explained lightheartedly. The other passengers shuffled past their seats exiting the cabin. "But they're a precious miracle."

"Yeah?" Buck said. "After thirty billion it's not called a precious miracle. It's called overpopulation."

The mother looked appalled but did not let him into the aisle before her, purposely taking her time. She led Buck off the flight at a snail's pace. When they exited the plane, Buck took full advantage and sped around the mother and child.

Stepping into the airport, Buck looked around for some sort of directional guide. He was surprised to see a woman holding a sign with his name. The stunning African American woman stood five foot eight inches tall including her two-inch heels. Her hair was straight and dyed a rust color with highlighted streaks racing through. The bangs swept across her forehead and over the carefully contoured eyebrows. Iridescent Confederate blue eye shadow highlighted the expressive half-moon dark green eyes. Her face was round and her bronzed full lips remained tightly closed.

"I'm Buck Miller," he called out with a wave of his hand, approaching the woman dressed in a black and white plaid shirt. Black boots that matched her open leather jacket crept halfway up her calves, and the slim legs of her blue denim jeans were tucked into them.

"Thank goodness you're here." Buck started talking nonstop. "I have this carry-on," he tapped the bag strapped across his chest, "and this one I'm dragging behind. I'm definitely going to need help with the other two bags. They're like this one, big and dark red, hard-shelled suitcases. I'm guessing they'll be the only two you'll see down there like this, but just in case my name is on the tags. There was a kid on that plane that wouldn't shut up and now I have a headache that won't stop! And be careful with the luggage, it's Rimowa."

The woman's face remained completely void of expression. Slowly she lowered the sign and let it hang at her side. With a deep breath she drew herself up to Buck's height, looking him directly in his hazel eyes, which were widening with surprise. The bronze-painted lips slowly disappeared as her nostrils flared, stretching outward. Her head began to rotate on her motionless shoulders.

"I'm sorry, but your headache is about to get worse," she said. Holding up a single finger with a stark white French-tipped manicure, she jabbed the tip into Buck's chest to emphasize every important point.

"I ain't The Help," she started. "Now, I may be of some help to some people at some time. And at some time in the future, *should* we become friends, I *may* be able to offer some help to you. Currently, I am the assistant to the governor of the glorious state of Florida. So, I am of help to him—which is why I am here. But I am not now, nor will I *ever* be, *The* Help. That means you can get your own damn bags. Oh Kay?"

Buck couldn't help but chuckle at the woman's attitude, a reaction that didn't seem to please her. He gave her his friendliest "first impression" smile, a large grin with half of his perfect teeth showing. Not knowing how to take the comment, Buck offered an awkward chuckle. With a slow breath he raised himself to his full five-foot-nine-inch height, running a hand over his orange-colored Ralph Lauren pullover.

"Let's start again." Buck held out his hand, ready for shaking. "Obviously, I'm Buck Miller."

Her sharp ivy-colored eyes cut a line down from his face to the still-extended hand. Hesitantly they moved downward, taking in the blue slacks and the black Prada loafers. The unimpressed glare slowly climbed its way back up until she met his eyes.

"Mmm-hmm," she hummed out and turned, taking a step away. "This way to baggage claim."

"Hey!" Calling after her, he reached out, taking hold of her shoulder.

Instantly her head snapped around until her half-moon eyes became full and glaring.

"I didn't get your name," Buck said, trying to hide the wavering in his voice.

"You didn't get it because you never asked me for it," she replied. "If you were polite enough to inquire, my name is Phynilla Jackson." She drummed her fingernails against the sign she still held in her hand. "But you weren't, so I never said. To avoid any confusion, you should know I'm not the driver either, and you're on your own for the luggage. Be careful with my jacket—it's Gucci!"

Phynilla knocked Buck's hand off her shoulder and led the way to baggage claim without once looking back. Despite the airport noise swelling around him, he distinctly heard her heeled boots clicking away on the airport tiles, echoing in her wake.

❖

The Town Car sped away from the airport as soon as Buck put the luggage in the trunk and got into the car. The sky was dark with thick gray clouds. After a few droplets, the sky let loose a downpour as they drove in a heavy, awkward silence. Buck and Phynilla sat in the backseat on opposite sides, against their respective car doors.

"It was sunny when we landed," Buck said, trying to make conversation.

"Welcome to Florida in September," Phynilla said. Her words were quick and short. "After Labor Day this happens every day during the afternoon. Pours down like this to where you practically can't see. Stops like a faucet being turned off and everything's sunny again."

As she spoke, the rain trickled to a stop. By the next mile the sun returned.

"What kind of name is Phynilla?" Buck said, trying to break the ice. "Is it Hispanic?"

"No," was the only word offered.

"Is it Filipino?"

"Do I look Filipino to you?" Her eyebrows arched with faux shock.

"Hey," Buck said. "I'm trying here. You could help me out." He folded his arms, pushing himself as far into the car seat as he could, gazing out the tinted window.

"It's a family name," Phynilla softly replied after a long pause and a heavy sigh. "My mama came up with it."

Buck said nothing, waiting for her to explain.

"My mama was a simple woman, not very well educated and a little hard of hearing. After my birth she was still groggy from the medications, and they asked her if she wanted her choice of ice cream. My mama thought they were offering baby names. She said: 'Give me Phynilla.' She thought it was a prettier name than Chocolate for a black girl."

Buck thought it best not to say a word and mentally recited the *Hamlet* soliloquy to fill the void. He looked at her, waiting for anything further to be said.

Phynilla nodded with a snort and a flicked eyebrow, approving of his silence. She turned away to look out the window.

"Thank God she wasn't offered Tutti Frutti," Buck said to the tinted glass. "You and Little Richard could have been best buds."

"I beg your pardon!" Phynilla snapped around, making a gesture toward him. "You are lucky that this seat belt is holding me back."

"I'm sorry," Buck said with a laugh. He put his palms up in front of him. "It was a joke waiting to be said."

Phynilla's eyes grew wide. Suddenly her entire demeanor shifted. Her shoulders relaxed and her face calmed down. Another breath caused an awkward, impish smile to creep across her lips like a baby troll doll.

"Thank goodness I ain't your mama," Phynilla said, her voice dripping with saccharine poison. She gave Buck's arm a playful slap and a demonically possessed grin. "You're so cute and original that I could forgive you anything. You know, I don't think anyone in all my thirty-seven years has ever made a joke about my name." She forced out an overly exaggerated squeal, slapping her knee and shoving Buck against the door.

"Children can be so kind about a silly thing like a name. And then you come along, so clever and all that! Let me tell you somethin'." Her body snapped to rigid attention and her voice iced over to a dull calm. The green flashed from her eyes as if a traffic light had changed color and her head tilted downward, causing her facial expression to grow darker in the car light.

"It ain't funny!"

"I hate to state the obvious," Buck suggested slowly. "But have you ever thought of changing it?"

"Why would I do that?" Phynilla looked at him as if he suggested regicide. "It's my name. The name that you possess helps to shape your life and who you become. My name is one-of-a-kind. It's unique and it is special. My name is as much a part of me as anything else I have done with my life. Can you say the same, *Buck*?"

The awkward silence returned and sat heavily on the car's backseat between them.

"What?" Buck finally said with irritation. "You keep staring at my pants like I put my jock on the outside of them. What's wrong with my pants?"

"I'm not sure where you're from but, child, you're in the South now, and colors like that just aren't usually worn by men. Plus, they are blue. And your shirt is orange."

"It isn't orange," Buck said defensively. "It's carrot, and my pants are turquoise."

"Carrot? Turquoise?" Phynilla repeated sarcastically. She shook her head with disbelief. "If people didn't know you were gay before…"

"Well, forgive me for playing with more than five colors in the Crayola box!"

"Brian." Phynilla leaned forward, speaking to the driver through the open dividing partition. "Don't take Fourth Avenue, there's a protest march going on there. Go down Duval instead."

"I haven't heard anything being mentioned, Ms. Jackson," Brian answered, his gray eyes reflecting in the rearview mirror. "And the governor usually keeps me informed of these things."

"*I* am the assistant to the governor. I am telling you there's going to be a march going down Fourth Avenue today."

Brian didn't answer and Phynilla sat back, looking out the window.

"I didn't mean to offend," Buck said quietly. "About your

name, and all. I just have this natural ability to instantly rub people wrong."

"You do it so well it must be a gift from God," Phynilla sneered. She took a deep breath, turning to face him. "I don't care if you are the biggest son of a bitch on the planet Earth. The governor speaks highly of you and that's all that matters."

"I was only the runner-up," Buck stated. "I lost out for congeniality."

"Mmm-hmm."

"Don't worry," Buck said confidently. "We'll find the boy."

Phynilla punched his leg. She jerked her head toward the partition window.

"Has something happened to the kid?" Brian asked.

"I guess the surprise is out now," Phynilla said. "We're planning on getting Alejandro a puppy. Buck is a friend of the governor's and happens to know several dog breeders in the area."

"The governor and I," Buck improvised, "have known each other many years. This is just the first time I've gotten a chance to visit."

"Welcome to Florida," Brian said. The sneer was heard clearly and the smirk reflected in the rearview mirror.

"Am I the only one visiting the property?" Buck asked. "I haven't been to Swan Lake in a long time."

"Lake Swan," Phynilla corrected. "It's Florida, not Tchaikovsky. There is security present. The workers should be finished."

"The joys of being an elected official, I guess."

"And there's Mrs. Truque," Brian volunteered.

The Town Car made a turn and glided softly to a halt. Ahead at the crosswalk, the road was blocked off, and two men in uniform stood guard. An officer approached and Brian lowered the window. An oppressive humidity rolled in despite the car's air-conditioning. Distant chanting could be heard approaching from down the street.

"What's going on?" Brian asked the officer.

"Some protest march," the officer said. There was a twang in his accent. "You're gonna have to turn your vehicle around and go another route."

"Can't you just get us across the street?" Brian asked.

"Sir," the officer continued. He accentuated his meaning by leaning on the car's windowsill. "I said, you're gonna have to turn your car around, and find an alternative route."

"Excuse me." Phynilla spoke up from the backseat. Her back window lowered with a hum, letting in more of the suffocating humidity. Reaching into her purse, she pulled out a business card and extended it through the window.

"This is the governor's car and we're on official business. We would appreciate it very much if you would direct us across the street. It would save us a lot of time and the governor would be most grateful."

The guard studied the card in his hand and then checked the license plate of the car. He stood up and looked across the vehicle toward a group of people approaching about two blocks down.

"Hold up," he called out to his lone companion. "Move those cones and let the governor's car go through."

Phynilla sat back as the tinted window hummed back up. "That would be the protest march that you didn't hear about, Brian," she said.

"Sorry, ma'am," Brian mumbled. "But I'm usually informed of these things and I heard nothin' about this one."

The police officers moved the cone barricades and waved the car forward. As the Town Car crossed the intersection, Buck could see the crowd coming toward them.

"I wonder what the protest is about," he muttered.

The car crossed and continued on its way.

"They aren't happy with the governor wanting to sign the Marriage Equality Bill," Phynilla answered into the window.

"R-65?" Buck jumped onto the sentence. "And who are 'they'?"

"The Pilgrim's Church of the Holy Trinity," Phynilla answered with a heavy sigh. She turned to face Buck. "It's a Southern Baptist church with a large African American congregation."

"And they are against equality?" Buck was aghast.

"The African American community in the South can be an extremely devout one," Phynilla said indignantly. "Many of them feel very strongly about homosexuality. As it is written in Leviticus 18:22: 'Thou shall not lie with a male as with a woman; it is an abomination.' "

Phynilla bobbed her head as if punctuating her sentence.

"Funny." Buck snickered back. "Ephesians 6:5 says, 'Slaves, obey your earthly masters with fear and trembling, with a sincere heart, as you would Christ.' I doubt they're so willing to uphold that one."

"You have quite the mouth on you," Phynilla said. "You know that?"

"Better men than you have told me."

"Please do not tell me I'm sitting here next to a bigot," Phynilla stated. Her head began to sway on her shoulders.

"I'm not a bigot," Buck protested. "I have slept with every race, religion, color, creed, or orientation out there, and all I can say is that it's all red when you slice them with an axe! You have a right to believe anything you want to, even if I don't agree with it."

"That's mighty nice of you," Phynilla said.

"What I mean is that I don't have an issue with anyone's religion, either," Buck said. "My issue only begins when someone starts to actively campaign against my civil rights. Then they are using religion as an excuse for bigotry. And I still wouldn't vote to have their inalienable rights taken away."

"And pray tell," Phynilla slyly asked, "you must have some prejudices. No one is exempt from that."

"I don't like children," Buck said, unashamed. "But that doesn't mean I would vote to hurt them. WC Fields was onto something when he said, 'Children are obscene and should not be heard.'"

He flashed a smile to illustrate his humor. Phynilla's sour expression failed to acknowledge it.

The Town Car turned off the road and onto one that wasn't paved yet. Trees lined the one-lane path except for the few dugout crescents to allow the rare oncoming car to pass. The car meandered its way as the trees began thinning out, then it came to a stop at the heavy metal gate blocking off any advance.

A guard stood on either side of the road, dressed in matching uniforms. The one on the left was noticeably shorter and heavier with dark brown hair peeking out from under the brim of his hat with the security logo centrally printed. The thinner man was blond and in much better shape. It was the heavier guard who walked toward the car and over to the driver's side.

"It's just me, Jimmy," Brian said as the car window lowered. "I'm with Ms. Jackson and a friend of the governor's."

Jimmy leaned in from a yard's distance onto the car door, bracing his hands on the open window frame. Lowering his head, he glanced into the backseat without bothering to take off his reflective sunglasses.

"You got an ID with you?" Jimmy said in a thick Southern drawl.

"Yeah," Buck said, reaching into his front pocket for his wallet.

"You can go ahead and give it to the other officer," Jimmy continued. The backseat window was lowered from Brian's driver control panel.

As the window lowered, it slowly revealed the crotch of the security guard standing by the car's door. The tight gray uniform with the blue stripe up the side fit the man's thighs quite snugly.

Buck said nothing, staring with his wallet in hand.

"As Lizzie Borden once said," Phynilla commented, slapping him in the arm, "don't make me axe you again! Give the man your ID."

Buck shook himself out of the momentary trance, fishing out the plastic card with his photo.

"Do I hand it over," Buck asked salaciously, "or do I stick it in your waistband like I'm tipping a stripper?"

The security guard took a step back before squatting down, a clipboard resting against the car door. The man stared with a stoic expression over his paperwork. Buck looked into the reflective sunglasses hovering over a Romanesque nose and bushy blond-brown mustache. The jawline was strong and clenched, with his chin holding a small centered dimple.

"Do you see me dancing?" the security guard asked in complete deadpan. "I'll take that."

"I bet you'd do it well." Buck handed over the plastic card. The officer jotted down a few notes before returning it.

"Go ahead," the blond officer called out. He stood up and away from the car.

The window hummed up quickly, leaving Buck to stare out through tinted glass. The two guards unlocked the gate and pulled it open, allowing the car to enter. As they drove by, Buck's vision was locked onto the blond officer.

"I wish I were in his land of cotton...drawers!" Buck said. He turned to look at Phynilla and jumped.

Phynilla's disturbed expression melted into something softer immediately after she caught hold of Buck's attention.

"When I was a little girl," she began as if telling a children's story, "my older brother CJ had this bull terrier named Jasper. He loved that dog, but Jasper was always sticking its nose into other people's personal business, if you get my meanin'. When I was about fourteen years old my brother went fishing for the entire day and left Jasper behind. Every time I sat down, that dog's nose was in my equator, and finally I had enough. I snuck into my mama's room and took out a few of her Valium, crushing 'em up and stickin' 'em into a hot dog. After I fed them to Jasper, I went into the kitchen and got Mama's good sharp knife."

"You killed the dog?" Buck said, appalled.

"Don't be hatin'," Phynilla said. "I liked that dog. I just had to fix something, if you get my meanin', Oh Kay!"

"Why are you telling me this?" Buck asked. He slid his wallet back into his pants.

"You just seem to remind me a bit of Ol' Jasper." Phynilla's smile crept across her closed lips.

The car pulled into a circular clearing about fifty yards in diameter, stopping on the right-hand side. Across from the loop's only entrance, a walking path began on the other side of three stumps to prevent any cars from passing. It led off around the driveway and circled back behind the trees. There were two other vehicles in the circle: a small black Volkswagen Jetta with a vanity license plate reading "HTCOCOA" and a medium-sized royal blue panel truck. Painted in the center of the truck's side was an explorer's ship with the words "UnCharted Construction" printed in yellow block letters above "Exploring your ideas."

The car was barely at a halt when Phynilla's seat belt was off and she was halfway out the door.

"I'm sure you can get your own Rimowa luggage. I'll see you at the house. Follow the path across the drive and around there. Don't dawdle." She slammed the door shut and quickly took off toward the path, disappearing around the curl of trees.

"I don't know why," Buck muttered, watching Phynilla disappear down the pathway, "but I'm feeling like Mary Todd Lincoln just after she's been shown to her theater seat."

Chapter Four

I don't suppose you'd give me a hand with the bags?" Buck asked, already knowing the answer. He flashed a cartoon smile. "Even if I say please?"

The driver got out of the Town Car with a smirk plastered on his round, pug-like face. He reached into his pocket, taking out his keychain. Pressing a button caused the trunk to open.

"There ya go." Brian leaned his plump frame against the car's side, folding his arms across his chest.

"That's all you can do?" Buck asked.

"So'ry," was the drawled response. It rolled out like a seal's bark.

"I'm guessing Florida is not a state of overachievers," Buck muttered as he went around to the rear of the car. He pulled out the bags, slamming the trunk harder than needed.

"Are you the governor's only driver?" asked Agent 98 as he pulled the luggage behind.

"Me and Howie," was the answer. "I usually do it, but when I'm not around Howie does."

"Do you drive anyone else?" Buck asked. He adjusted the bag's strap across his chest. "Have any celebrity gossip, or is this one of the perks of being the governor of Florida?"

"Phynilla has her own car." Brian ignored the comment with

a look of disdain. He pointed to the black Jetta with the vanity plates.

"Truque?" Brian answered with a sneer. "It's French. She likes to remind people of that."

"Mrs. Truque, then," Buck said with a heavy sigh. "Did she have her own car?"

"Sometimes I'd have to drive her into town," Brian said. "Sometimes she'd have her own car. I think it was one of those Zippo rentals."

"And what do you do if the governor doesn't need a ride someplace?"

Brian smiled and spread his arms. "You're lookin' at it."

"Nice work if you can get it," Buck said. He pulled at his shirt, the perspiration causing it to cling to his chest.

"Yeah," Brian agreed, drawing the word out into two syllables.

Buck started up the path holding a luggage handle in each hand. The grass, still wet from the afternoon shower, didn't make it easier, caking mud onto the wheels. As he turned the corner around the curl of trees, the path ended, presenting a sign offering two options. Going to the left meant following the trail up a small incline and around the trees. Buck could make out parts of the house through the thick grove.

To take the right-hand path was to go toward the dock. His eyes followed the walkway down toward the water, where the grass gave way to a dock. Houses dotted the coastline with large spaces of property between them.

"Even if they swam up," Buck concluded, looking at the stretches of sandy beaches, "there's no way anyone could come or go without being seen."

The sounds of high-pitched barking pulled him from his thoughts. Turning around, he saw small dogs leaping up to see over the grass and charging toward him. The first two to clear the tall grass were no bigger than Chihuahuas, except the breed wasn't easily identified. Each dog wore a knitted outfit around its tiny body with holes cut for the ears and tail. One was dressed like a tiger and the other, a lion.

"You are just so cute!" Buck laughed at the approaching, yappy animals.

A third animal leapt out of the grass. Its dark brown face and snout stood out in contrast to the white rabbit outfit it was wearing. Long knitted ears awkwardly weighted down the dog so that when it ran too fast, it tripped over its headdress. The three animals circled around Buck, barking incessantly.

"Such ferocious creatures." He stooped down, trying to pet each one as they barked excitedly, competing for his attention.

"You are so sweet!" Buck cooed to the yapping creatures. "I could just pick you up and take you home!"

"I wouldn't advise it," said a voice from behind him. The barrel of a rifle pressed between his shoulder blades. "Put your hands where I can see 'em, and step away from the dogs."

The voice was older and female. She pushed on the rifle to emphasize her insistence. The dogs stopped barking as soon as they heard the woman speak.

Buck raised his hands and slowly stood up. The dogs deserted him, running back to their mistress.

"Turn around slow," she commanded. "I wouldn't want to put a hole into something so pretty."

"I'm flattered," Buck answered. "Really I am, but I'm here to see the governor."

The woman standing behind the rifle was a little shorter than him, but Buck wasn't about to point it out. Her blond hair brushed off her forehead was liberally streaked with gray, giving her a regal appearance.

"Of course you are," she said, unconvinced. "What's your name and what are you doing here?"

"My name's Buck Miller and the governor should be expecting me. I just arrived with Phynilla Jackson?"

The woman seemed unimpressed and kept the firearm steadily pointed at him.

"Can I at least put my arms down?" Buck asked. "I'm starting to feel like Evita."

"I won't cry for you until we get up to the house and can sort all of this out," the woman stated. "Let's hope you're telling the truth."

"What should I do with my bags?"

"Leave 'em for now," the woman commanded. "You can either come back for them or we'll send them with you to the morgue."

She flicked the rifle toward the upper path. Buck took a few steps forward and she moved behind him, the barrels poised in position. The dogs trotted by their feet as if escorting a prisoner to the wall.

The path ended and they began walking across the open grass toward the front of a ranch-style house. The subtle incline of the damp lawn made walking difficult in his Prada loafers. As he took a large step forward, the tip of his shoe slipped on the grass.

Buck fell forward, spinning himself around. Sliding down, he wrapped his feet around the woman's ankles and twisted with his legs. She was caught by surprise and fell backward. The firearm flew free from her hands, landing two yards away on the grass. Agent 98 leapt to his feet, the dogs barking and nipping at his legs.

The woman was on her back and rolling to her side. She was wearing a pair of pastel blue shorts and a pale peach top. Ankle socks were tucked into a pair of dirty white sneakers.

"My God!" she cried out, curling in pain. "You monster! You broke my hip!"

All three of the costumed dogs ran over barking with concern, and as a warning for Buck to keep his distance.

Agent 98 looked after the rifle tossed to the side. She made no movement toward it. The woman lay on her right side clutching at her left hip, crying in agony. Hesitantly he took a step toward her and when she didn't notice he took another, ignoring her wail of pain.

"I'm going to the house and calling someone," Buck said. He bent down toward her.

The woman's right arm flew up, connecting with Buck's jaw. The surprise force of the blow sent him reeling backward.

"I don't think so, sucker," she quipped, leaping to her feet. The dogs were already running after him.

Buck landed on his back for a quick moment. One of the pups bit into his sleeve and he knocked it backward. It went rolling away in a somersault, yelping as he jumped back to his feet.

"Oh no you did not!" said the woman.

She was standing two yards away, the rifle lying a short distance from them. They both saw the firearm and simultaneously made a move for it. As she reached for the gun Buck tugged at her ankle, causing her to fall short. She rolled onto her back, bringing her knees to her chest, and as he approached she let go and kicked out.

The flats of her feet collided into Buck's stomach, knocking all the air from his body. Falling back on the ground, he lay there gasping for air as the dogs leapt on his chest and arms. Two of them growled while the last barked in a high-pitched tone.

A shrill whistle cut the air. The dogs jumped off, barking and running back to their mistress. The darker dog dressed like a rabbit stood still, continuing to snarl and yelp.

"Shut up, Jenny," the woman yelled at the dog. It stopped for a brief moment before resuming. Pointing the rifle squarely at Buck's chest, the woman came closer.

"Now," she said. "We're going to try this again. And mind you, you make another move like that and you'll be full of more holes than a politician's promise."

Buck stood up, raising his arms once again.

"You're making a mistake here," Buck said over the one

dog's howls. "Really, if you aim that gun at the dog and shoot, we'd all be better off."

"Shut up, Jenny!" she answered. "The little bitch may be a nuisance, but I'm the only one allowed to berate her. We've had enough talking. Now walk up to the house, nice and slow."

CHAPTER FIVE

A s they approached the elongated house, Phynilla stood on the front porch to welcome them. A smug look was plastered on her face and her arms were folded across her chest. Muffled sounds of hammering and electric drills came from somewhere behind the residence.

"That's fine," Phynilla said. She smiled, welcoming the approaching entourage. "I'll take it from here."

"Then you *do* know this scallywag," said the woman from behind the rifle.

"He's a friend of the governor's. Buck, what's wrong with you? Didn't you tell her?" Phynilla said with faux shock. "I thought he was right behind me. We must have gotten separated. I told you not to dawdle. Sorry to take you away from your watch, Countess."

"Quite all right," she said grandly. "As long as everyone is safe."

The rifle was lowered from Buck's shoulders. He heard another shrill whistle and the dogs ran after her with a round of excited barking.

"Who in the hell is that crazy bitch?" Buck asked, putting his arms down to his sides.

"The dog that wouldn't shut up?" Phynilla sarcastically answered. "That's Jenny in the rabbit outfit. The Earle and

Marquise are in the tiger and lion outfits, respectively. They're hairless Chinese dogs."

"Funny. *Not!*" Buck said, turning around and watching the retreating figure. "Did you say that woman is a countess?"

"Countess Margareta Theresa Valois Stewart Rosenblatt, to be exact," Phynilla explained. She stepped aside, holding the front door open. "She's the governor's aunt come for a visit. She only arrived here this morning."

"And tell me exactly why she has a rifle?"

They entered the foyer of the house. A kitchen ran to the right, leading farther back into the house, and a hallway disappeared off to the left.

"She's keeping watch for the eagles," Phynilla explained with a deadpan expression. "So they don't swoop down and carry off one of the precious little puppies."

"You can't be serious."

"We should be so lucky," Phynilla answered with a bob of her head.

"That's insane!" Buck declared.

"Don't let her hear you say that, or you'll be back staring down the barrel of a rifle."

"Are eagles even native to these parts?" Buck asked. "When was the last time an eagle was even seen in Florida?"

"They haven't been seen in over ten years, Oh Kay?" Phynilla said with a direct, hushed voice. "But we told her there were sightings not far away. We gave her a rifle filled with blanks and set her out on the lawn, out of our way. Governor Reyes is under extreme pressure right now, as your visit will attest. Our instructions were explicit. No one was supposed to know Alejandro was kidnapped."

"Where did you tell her the boy was?" Buck asked, incredulous and impressed.

"As far as anyone knows, he left early this morning for a camping trip with friends. Besides," Phynilla carefully explained, "no one is getting up to this house without our knowledge again. Not with that noisy alarm-bitch Jenny out there."

"Evidently."

They moved through the kitchen and into a casual den with a couch, two reclining chairs, and a television. Standing next to the chairs stood two men engaged in conversation.

"Angel," snapped the shorter of the two men. "What happened to the toilet that we brought in two days ago?"

Governor Miguel Reyes was dressed in a black suit, with an open jacket covering a royal blue shirt. A melon-shaped head was topped with a thick mass of curly black hair. A scruffy goatee surrounded a pair of thin lips.

"We couldn't get it installed properly," the foreman explained. "I had to send that one back this morning and now we're waiting for another to be delivered. I'll get the window installed today."

The foreman stood at six feet and three inches tall, but because of his muscular frame, he seemed to tower over the stouter governor despite only a three-inch difference in height.

"We'll have it finished this weekend, I promise."

The governor studied the foreman for a moment, then nodded.

"Gracias."

The two men shook hands and the foreman started off. Buck took note of the handsome features of the worker: the built body, the dark eyes, and the rectangular head with the cropped hair.

"You must be Buck Miller."

The governor's voice pulled Buck from his jarhead fantasy.

"Governor," Buck said, extending his hand. "It's an honor and a pleasure."

"Thank you," he answered softly. His dark brown eyes were soft and welcoming.

"I'm here to bring Alejandro home," Buck said. "I'll need your cooperation, but with a little luck we'll have him home to you as soon as possible. Now, is there somewhere we can talk without worry of being overheard?"

"There's my home office." He pointed to one of two closed doors on opposite walls behind them. "Or my bedroom."

"I've always had better luck in bedrooms than offices," Buck answered. "Lead the way."

A framed lithograph picture of a seventeenth-century innkeeper greeted all those entering the master bedroom. An index card tucked into the bottom left corner read in a child's scrawl: "To Papi—Master of the House."

"Does that make you the keeper of the zoo?" Buck said, pointing to the picture, making reference to *Les Miserablés*.

"We went to see the musical six months ago," Governor Reyes said. "It was his first one and he loved it. I think the theater bug might have bitten him hard. Alejandro gave me that for my birthday."

The room was spacious with a king-sized bed against one wall and a set of sliding closet doors running the length of the opposite one. Behind a pair of drawn shades, a set of glass doors led out to a porch.

"Were you here or at the Capitol when Alejandro was kidnapped?" Buck asked. The three of them entered the room and the bedroom door was closed.

"I was in my office in Tallahassee," Miguel answered. "It's a twenty-minute drive and I'm usually at the office by eight a.m."

"Who was here at the time?"

"I'm not sure," he responded. "Phynilla?"

"I was still on my way here," Phynilla explained. "The countess didn't arrive for another two hours. So I think only Mrs. Truque and Alejandro were here."

"What is Mrs. Truque's first name?" Buck asked. "Doesn't anybody use it?"

Phynilla and Miguel looked at each other and, after a brief beat, simultaneously chuckled.

"No," Miguel said. "I guess we usually don't. It's Barbe if

you need to know, but most people have always called her Mrs. Truque."

"Always?" Buck asked. "How long has she been working for you?"

Miguel thought carefully for a moment before answering. "It must be about ten years now. She started working for us as a summer tutor for Alejandro. He's always been an advanced kid when it comes to his schooling."

"What time did you get here?" Buck turned to Phynilla.

"Not until later," she answered. "Mrs. Truque called me and I drove here immediately. It must have been about nine forty-five by the time I arrived. The countess got here about thirty minutes later."

"You didn't know she was coming?" Buck asked Miguel.

"She rarely announces it when she does," he explained. "Most of the family tries to avoid her. She can be quite eccentric."

"I've discovered that," Buck said with a snort. "Who first discovered Alejandro was missing?"

"Mrs. Truque," Phynilla answered. "Alejandro went inside to get some sunscreen and she was waiting on the dock, on the boat. When he didn't come back she went inside and found his sandals neatly lined up outside the door, and a note on his bed."

Miguel crossed the room and opened the bedside nightstand. He returned holding out a rectangular piece of paper. A faint design of the interlocked Tragedy-Comedy masks was centered on the page of the stationery notepad. Uneven block letters were carefully hand-printed in heavily pressed pencil.

We have your son
Tell no one!
Kill R-65 or
We kill your kid.
We will be in touch
You have one week

"Any recognition of the handwriting?" Buck asked, studying the note.

"No."

"Have they been in touch yet?"

"No," Miguel said. "It's been pure hell. There's nothing I can do but this incessant waiting. I feel so helpless."

"I think I need to speak to this Truque woman," Buck said. "Where is she?"

"I told you," Phynilla said. "She received an emergency call and had to leave."

"What kind of call?" Buck asked suspiciously.

"I don't know. I was not there to receive it."

"She called me afterward," Miguel interjected. "It was a death in her family and she needed to go back home."

"And where's that?" Buck asked with interest.

"Somewhere outside of Paris," he answered. "I can't remember the name of the city."

"So your son is kidnapped," Buck reiterated. "The only witness receives a phone call and must leave before anyone else appears on the scene? Does anyone else find this a little bit peculiar?"

"Mr. Miller, I know Mrs. Truque very well—"

"But not well enough to call her by a first name?" Buck snapped back.

"Look," Miguel firmly said. "I've known her for many years. She's been a wonderful employee, and I know it's odd not to use her first name, but she's like a member of the family."

"The thing I find odd is that no one else was here," Buck stated. "What about the security at the gate? When did they arrive?"

"They got here at nine a.m.," Miguel answered. "Alejandro was already gone. The construction workers never show up before ten a.m. They were all here when either of us arrived."

"Does anyone else have the gate key?"

"No."

"What aren't you telling me?" Buck asked. "Why isn't this woman on your radar?"

"Mr. Miller," Governor Reyes said with a confused look, "I already told you."

"No offense, sir. But when a child is kidnapped, no matter what the reasons, the culprit is more often than not someone known. We can't rule anyone out at this point."

Buck was silent before another thought occurred to him.

"Why wasn't Alejandro in school?" he asked. "This is after Labor Day already, don't most schools start by now?"

"Alejandro is in a private school in New York," Miguel responded. "His school doesn't start for another two weeks."

The sounds of Beethoven's Fifth Symphony rang out from his pants pocket.

"Sorry," Miguel said. He withdrew the phone.

Buck nodded and walked to the other end of the bedroom, giving the governor privacy for his call. Intrigued by a framed photo on the wall, he moved toward it for a better look, when he heard the governor's voice.

"Alejandro! Is that you?"

CHAPTER SIX

At the sound of the governor's voice an immediate silence strangled the room. All heads snapped around and stared at Miguel, his hand shaking, holding the cell phone to his ear. Emotional pain twisted across his face, pinching his cheeks, sucking in his lips, and locking his jaw. A vein throbbed on the side of his neck.

"Alejandro," Miguel whispered hoarsely. "Is that you?"

Governor Reyes held the phone away, studying the screen. When he slid his finger across, the tinny sound of a boy's voice came through the speaker.

"...Me, *Papi*."

"Are you okay, Alejandro?" Miguel pleaded. "Are you hurt, *m'ijito*?"

"No," said the frightened voice. "I'm just scared."

"Don't be afraid. Be strong. You'll be home soon, I promise."

"I'm trying to be brave," the boy said. He took a deep breath and spoke slowly. "I'm doing my best to follow Collins's Code."

"What?" Miguel asked. "Alejandro?"

The sounds of the phone shuffling on the other end echoed through the speaker.

"Listen closely," said an electronically altered voice. "If you want to see your son alive you will veto R-65 before next weekend."

"If you hurt one hair on my son's head, *hijo de puta...*"

"Sticks and stones, Governor," the voice chided. "You're in no position to make threats. One week, or the next time you see Alex will be in the morgue!"

The phone went dead.

"Alejandro! Alejandro!" Miguel pleaded.

Buck snatched the phone from the governor's hand.

"What are you doing?"

He ignored the shouting and slid his finger across the screen, punching in several digits on the keypad.

"Agent 98 here," he said into the phone. He looked at the screen and punched in four digits before returning the phone to his ear. "Trace the last call made to this number. Call me back on my phone ASAP."

He pressed several digits on the phone pad. The screen lit up and the phone rebooted, erasing all traces of his codes.

"What's going on?" Miguel asked.

"Our best chances of tracing that call are within the first few minutes," Buck explained. "The longer we wait, the more corrupt the original signal gets and the more difficult it is to track."

Audra McDonald's powerful soprano voice sounded from Buck's pocket. He snatched out his phone and held it to his ear.

"What can you tell me?" Buck waited, holding a finger up to keep the others silent. "Can you narrow that down?"

Miguel turned away and sat on the edge of the bed. His head fell into his hands, his fingers wringing through his hair.

"Get it to the lab and get it checked out," Buck was saying. "I doubt you'll find anything but here's hoping they get sloppy."

Buck ended the call. Seeing the anxiety growing in the room, he snapped into action.

"Phynilla," he ordered. "Get the governor some paper and a pen so he can write down every word of the conversation. Miguel, I need you to be as precise as you can possibly be, all right?"

Miguel nodded. Phynilla handed him a torn open envelope and a pen, and he began writing.

"Any reason why they'd call your cell phone and not your home phone?" Buck asked.

"This number is unlisted," Miguel said. "My cell phone is how people reach me when I'm here."

Agent 98 took the note from him and read over it.

"Did you notice anything odd?" Buck asked. "Did Alejandro sound strange or coerced into saying something?"

"They called him Alex," Miguel said after a moment. "Nobody calls him that except for me and Mrs. Truque. And that's only when we're mad at him."

"Are you sure of that?" Buck pounced on the detail.

"Very," Miguel answered. "Alejandro doesn't like being called by that name."

"What is 'Collins's Code'?" Buck pointed to the transcription.

"I have no idea."

"Why would your son say that?" Buck pushed.

"I don't know!" Miguel exploded. He stood up and paced the room, stomping across the carpet. "I don't know what it is. I only know that my son is gone! I only know that I'm going to find the sons of bitches who did this, and when I do I'm going to rip off their heads!"

"Calm down, Governor," Phynilla said. She placed a hand on his shoulder, gently pulling him back.

Miguel shook it off with an irritated shrug and exhaled deeply. He closed his eyes for a moment, controlling his frustrations with another slow breath.

"Mr. Miller," Governor Reyes said with an air of desperation. He looked as if he were on the verge of tears. "Is there *anything* good you can tell us?"

"The call was bounced between several towers, making it impossible to pinpoint," Buck explained. "But the call was domestic. And we can tell it most likely came from within a fifty-mile radius."

"How's that good news?"

"If the call came from inside that radius," Buck said slowly, "most likely that means the kidnappers are also within fifty miles, and so is Alejandro."

"Then we need to organize a manhunt!" Miguel said. His eyes blazed with fury.

"No!" Buck said. "The last thing you need to do is react to their threats."

"That's easy for you to say," Miguel said snidely. "It's not your son."

"No," Buck said firmly. "He's not. But the best chance you have to see him alive again is by working with me. And I'm telling you that a publicized manhunt is the surest way to get Alejandro killed."

The statement silenced everything else. Buck took a quick breath and pushed on, taking advantage of the governor's momentary calm.

"It is very important that you appear like nothing out of the ordinary has happened," Buck instructed. "You can do the most good right now by throwing all of your anger and strength into passing R-65. It's too important an issue to let fall by the wayside."

Governor Reyes got ready to shout something and caught himself before speaking a word. Staring into Buck's hazel eyes, he took a deep breath, letting the flames in his cheeks calm down.

"I feel so helpless," he finally managed to whisper.

"I know," Buck said, placing a hand on his shoulder. "It's not going to be easy, but you're going to have to stay strong. I need you to do that. For Alejandro."

Miguel Reyes nodded in silence.

"What if you're wrong, Mr. Miller?" he asked from desperation. "What then?"

Buck was silent for an instant.

"I don't know," he replied, perplexed. "It's not happened. I thought I was wrong once but was mistaken."

"Oh Lord, it's getting thick in here," Phynilla moaned.

"This picture here," Buck said, crossing back to the frame

on the wall. He removed it, holding the frame out in his hand. "When was this taken?"

Miguel and Phynilla stepped forward, pushing together to see the photograph. In it a small group of people all stood at different heights constructing a human totem pole. Next to them was the beach house in a more worn-down shape.

"That was about two weeks ago," Phynilla answered first.

"That was the day the construction was started," Miguel said. "Alejandro wanted a before-and-after shot."

"Okay," Buck said, pointing to the photo. He started at the bottom and worked his way to the tallest. "That's obviously Alejandro. Then there's Phynilla, and there's you, Miguel. So who is this?"

His finger landed below the face of a blurred figure. What could be seen was a woman with blond hair pulled behind her head and wearing a pair of sunglasses. Her head seemed to float above Miguel's. While everyone was looking straight ahead with a comic expression, she was distracted, her face turning away and the picture capturing a blurry figure.

"That's Barbe Truque," Phynilla answered.

"Why is she so blurry?" Buck asked. "It's like watching Lucille Ball in the movie musical *Mame*."

Miguel took a hold of the picture frame and looked at it closely.

"It looks like something was spilled on the picture," he said.

"Do you have any other pictures of her?" Buck asked.

"No," Miguel answered, looking rather puzzled. "She's always been camera-shy and is usually the one taking the photo."

"Is she wearing heels?" Buck asked. "You're barely bent at all, Miguel, and she's standing above you."

"No," Phynilla answered. "She's tall is all."

Audra's soprano rang out once more. Buck answered his phone, taking a few steps away.

"Tell me something good," Buck sang. "Can't you get any prints off it, Muffin? Okay. Well, at least that's something. What?

Send me the address and I'll be there in ninety minutes. *Ciao*, Muffin."

He ended the call, addressing the others.

"We traced the signal to a disposable cell phone," Buck hesitantly said. "It was found in a Dumpster in south Tallahassee."

Miguel's eyes sparked into thought. They speedily moved back and forth in their sockets.

"That's closer to town than where you said they were earlier," he reported. "Does that mean that Alejandro is somewhere in Tallahassee?"

"There's always a chance," Buck said. "But for now we can't guarantee that. Not yet."

Miguel sank back down on the bed's edge. "I feel so helpless."

"Here's something you can do for me now," Buck said. "How about showing me to my room. I'll grab my bags and maybe take a quick shower. How do you put up with this humidity? Can someone take me into Tallahassee in about an hour or so? I need to pick up my car."

Miguel looked at Phynilla, who immediately shook her head.

"I have errands I need to do. Personal errands," she stressed.

"I'll have Brian drive you on his way out," Miguel said. "In the meantime, follow me and we'll get your bags."

"I'll get them," Phynilla said. "I'll put them on the porch before I leave."

"Thank you," Buck said.

Miguel led Buck to the other end of the house. There were two bedrooms across from each other at the end of the hallway. As they approached, the sounds of construction increased.

"This is the new bathroom that's being installed," Miguel said. He patted the newly installed door between the two bedrooms. "This is Alejandro's room, which my aunt is currently using."

Miguel opened the door to the warm scent of sandalwood perfume and clean dog. The furniture consisted of a twin bed against the wall and a writing desk with computer flashing a "WICKED, the musical" screen saver. Several theatrical posters hung on the walls, all from the Seminole Players Community Theater. Buck walked over to the desk and subtly opened the drawer.

"Buck," Miguel called to him. "Let me go make your arrangements with Brian before it gets too late. Your room is across the hall. It's comfortable and was Mrs. Truque's. If you need anything, don't hesitate to ask."

"Sure," Buck said. "Thank you."

He waited until Miguel was down the hall before darting back into the room. Moving to the desk, he opened the drawer and tore off the top paper on the notepad. On it was the faded image of drama masks.

Leaving the bedroom, Buck took a look in the newly constructed bathroom. The tiles were polished from not being stepped on, and the glass-encased shower still had Styrofoam in the corners of the door. The window frame was empty, covered in thick opaque plastic. Sliding off his shoes, he stepped inside.

"This is going to be beautiful when it's finished," he muttered.

Standing in the middle of the room, he looked around at the detail. Noticing the Styrofoam, he leaned forward and reached to remove it. His socks slipped on the new tile and he lost his balance, falling forward and catching himself on the glass shower stall.

Something tore through the plastic covering. It landed with a thump in the painted drywall opposite, followed by another.

Buck instinctively fell to the floor. Looking up, he saw the plastic pulled away from the taped siding. Following the line of fire he saw two small holes in the fresh paint.

"Hey," someone called from the outside. "Anybody in there?"

"Yeah," Buck yelled back.

He stood to find the shadow of a construction worker on the

other side of the plastic-covered window frame. A gloved hand punched through, tearing down the plastic.

"I am so sorry, *amigo*," said the short and round Hispanic man. His eyes were wide with surprise. "I didn't know you were here."

"You almost hit me with your gun, there," Buck said. He took the two strides across the room and pointed to the holes.

"I will have that taken care of immediately. So sorry, *señor*." The man nodded and disappeared on the other side of the wall.

Buck inspected the holes. Using his keys he dug out two titanium nail bolts. He put them into his pocket when another worker appeared at the window. This was the more handsome one he had seen talking to the governor.

"Hey, dude," he called in through the window. "Are you all right?"

"Yeah," Buck said. "You don't have to call me dude."

"My guy told me what happened and I wanted to make sure you're not hurt?"

"I'm okay," Buck said. His surliness melted the more he looked at the handsome man.

"Cool. Punch it in if we're good." He held his fist out, knuckles bared.

"We're good," Buck said.

"You're leaving me hanging, dude?" The worker's fist remained in midair.

"Don't call me dude," Buck said. He turned to leave, speaking over his shoulder. "And I don't punch knuckles."

"I bet you punch doughnut holes."

Buck spun around to see the man already gone. He stared after, glaring out the window, the torn plastic hanging limply from the empty frame. The worker was gone and Agent 98 left the room.

He felt relaxed the moment he entered the room he'd been assigned. It felt warm and inviting as he threw his shoes in the corner and lay on the bed.

"Osiris," Buck said into his phone's speaker. "Wake me in forty-five minutes."

"Alarm set for forty-five minutes," said the male enhanced voice.

As he lay down on the pillow, a familiar scent crept into his nose. It was something distant, barely noticeable, but not something he was fond of either. As he closed his eyes, recognition struck, bringing a smile to his face. There were hints of amber in the fading perfume. Mrs. Truque and his "frenemy" fellow agent Noxia wore a similar scent.

CHAPTER SEVEN

"Brian," Buck said from the rear passenger seat. He looked at his watch, his foot pressing an imaginary gas pedal. "It's already six forty-five. Is there any way we can speed it up a bit?"

"So'ry," Brian said. "If I get caught speedin', I lose my job. Besides, traffic is slow. It always is on a game night."

"What kind of game are we talking about?" Buck said with piqued interest.

"The 'Noles, of course," he answered proudly.

"The what?"

"Florida State University Seminoles," Brian said. "This is football season."

"Oh." Buck immediately lost interest. "How far is Restaurant Row from here?"

"About two, three, four blocks at most."

"Fine," Buck said, his impatience getting the better of him. "Just pull over and let me off here."

"All righ' by me," Brian said and signaled to get over. He pulled to the curb and put on his flashing lights.

"Thanks," Buck said, getting out of the car.

Standing on the curb, he watched Brian drive away. Double-checking the earlier texted address, he wandered up the street until he came to the alley turn-off proclaiming itself "Restaurant Row."

Scanning the restaurants and cafés on both sides of the alleyway, Buck meandered among the groups of people. Halfway down he saw the desired location. As he made his way over, Buck nonchalantly scanned the crowds and surrounding cafés. Something on the opposite side caught his eye, distracting him, causing him to slow his pace. He craned his neck, trying for another glimpse and then, with a shake of his head and a brief shrug, dismissed the incident and started for the Mockingbird Café for his date with Muffin.

"I thought you'd be outside for sure," Buck said. He sat down at the table for four, opposite the pear-shaped man. "Especially here in sunny Florida."

"It's night and I prefer to talk to you in private," Agent 69 said. Keeping with his dressing in black tradition, his suit was made of linen. He gave Buck a once-over, studying his choice of clothing. "You do know that orange and blue are the rival team Gator colors, right?"

"It's not orange and blue," Buck said with an exasperated sigh. "It's carrot and turquoise. Really, didn't anyone read the color names in the Crayola box?"

"You're bound to attract unwanted attention, to say the least." He folded his hands, resting them on the tabletop.

"I doubt anyone is confusing me for a college boy," Buck said. "Despite my youthful appearance and demeanor."

"Others would say childish and immature behavior."

"Others can bite me," Buck concluded.

"Did you get settled in at Lake Swan?"

"Every time I hear that I think the person who named it must be dyslexic."

"Really," Agent 69 said with a sarcastic lilt. "You think that *every* time?"

"Give me a break, Muffin," Buck moaned. "I'm not acclimated yet to the South. I'm still a free thinker."

"Very nice." The pear-shaped man turned to the waitress. "I'll have the fried chicken, please."

"Make that two," Buck said. "And a lemon drop, please."

"I'm so'ry, sugar," the waitress said in a saccharine tone. "But we don't serve liquor. I can get you a lemonade if you'd like."

"That'll be fine," Buck answered, deflated. "And when you get a moment, may I borrow a pencil?"

"Sure, hon." The woman walked off to place the order.

"No liquor, Muffin?" Buck said. "Now I know why there's no one here while other places are packed."

"Which also gives us a little privacy to discuss your assignment. What have you learned so far, Agent 98?"

"The first thing is simple." Buck leaned back in his chair, crossing his legs at the knees and throwing an arm over the backing. "It's an inside job."

"Here ya go." The waitress dropped off a stump the size of a golf pencil.

"Why do you say that?" Agent 69 asked, his gray eyes narrowing as they studied him.

"More often than not," Buck continued, reaching into his pocket and taking out the paper he'd taken from Alejandro's pad, "these kinds of kidnappings are inside jobs. The kid was taken from the property. Fact. The security guards weren't on duty yet but the front gate was still locked. Fact. The note was left on the kid's bed. Fact. And they called him by the name Alex. That's a name people don't use with the kid, from what I've been told. Everything happened early, so it had to be someone who knew the grounds or knew the schedule of those working and living there."

"That hardly leads to a conclusion of an inside job."

"If you'd let me finish," Buck said. As he talked he gently shaded the paper with the side of the pencil's dull point. "Let's look at the gate first. Why lock the gate? If you were a kidnapper, would you take the time to get out of the car and lock the gate behind you? That would give a bigger chance of the security catching you, especially at that time of the morning. My guess is that either the boy was still on the property at the time, or they got him off property, locking the gate either out of habit or to pretend like nothing was out of the ordinary."

"That doesn't really help much now, does it?" Agent 69 drolly replied.

"Then there's this. I found a pad of this stationery in the kid's drawer."

Agent 98 finished shading the paper and slid it across the table. Incomplete if not clear imprints stood out in the gray coloring.

"It's the same paper as the one left by the kidnappers. You can even make out a few of the words from the note itself. They used paper from the boy's room."

"Okay."

"Muffin!" Buck exclaimed in quiet tones from across the table. "What kidnapper doesn't bring their own ransom note? Either this was an inside job, or the kidnapping was a last-minute decision. Judging from the factors, I'm guessing it was planned out."

"I fail to see how it *proves* anything," Muffin said. "If you remember the JonBenet Ramsey case, I believe the ransom note came from inside the house there as well. Nothing was ever proven and the case remains unsolved."

Buck coughed, raising his eyebrows and looking away with a sardonic expression. The waitress arrived with two plates of fried chicken, mashed potatoes, and green beans.

"Enjoy," she said. She flashed a smile before walking away.

"If you think it's an inside job," Agent 69 asked, "then whom do you suspect?"

"It's a no-brainer," Buck said. He took a big bite of chicken, making sounds of appreciation. "One thing I will say—"

"You've never only said one thing," Muffin interrupted.

"Good one," Buck commented. He spoke around voracious bites of food. "I will say that there's no better comfort food than in the South. As the saying goes, 'fat equals flavor,' which I'm guessing explains the size of the average Floridian. The answer to your question is Barbe Truque."

It took Agent 69 to replay the conversation, finding the previous thread.

"Why do you say it's her?" Muffin asked. He took another bite of chicken.

"I'm surprised no one else has fingered her," Agent 98 said. "She's one of the few people on the property when the boy goes missing. And she has to leave the country mysteriously right after? Maybe it's just my suspicious nature, but nobody seems to find this peculiar but me."

"If you read your notes," Agent 69 said with a paternal reprimand, "you might see that she's been a close member of the family for over a decade."

"And to use your own example," Buck said, matching Muffin's expression and tone, "both Ramsey parents were investigated for the kidnapping and murder of their daughter."

"Touché," Muffin concluded. "But if Truque is behind it, why now? She's must have known Miguel was gay before this, so what was the trigger that made her decide this was the time?"

"Maybe legalization of gay marriage was the breaking point for her?" Buck suggested. "It's the new sensation that's sweeping the nation. Maybe it was one state too many that finally woke up? Who knows the way a demented mind works?"

He finished his meal and pushed his plate aside.

"I'd think you would better than most," Muffin replied with a wry smile. He picked up his phone to send a text message.

"That's kind of you," Buck replied, missing the entendre. "Any luck on the cell phone? Any prints? Traces?"

"Nope," Agent 69 said. "They're called 'disposable' for a reason."

"It really doesn't make sense. They think about disposable phones, but not a ransom note. It just doesn't add up."

"Says the man who can't count to twenty-one without being completely nude."

"Zing," Buck said. His cell phone chimed with a message delivery. "Okay, now on to the good stuff. Where do I pick up my car?"

"Coincidentally," Muffin said, putting down his phone. He pushed his plate away, signaling for the check. "I just sent you the address. You'll find it within a short walk, parked on the street. It's a dark blue car. You should have no problems finding it."

"So what's been done to it?" Buck asked. His eyes narrowed. "Ejection seat? Guns that shoot out the exhaust pipe? Knives popping out of the tires to cut the wheels on another car? Come on, tell me!"

"You know when you get excited like that," said Muffin, keeping a stoic expression, "you get little lines by the sides of your eyes. There and there."

Buck sat back, glaring.

"You're not really funny, you know?"

"Oh," Muffin said with a satisfied grin. The waitress dropped off the check. "I'm a laugh riot."

"Tell me what's been done to the car."

Agent 69 reached into his pocket and took out a single key on a square black holder. He dangled it between them.

"I'll tell you what," Muffin said. "Why don't you get into the car and call me. It'll be a lot easier to explain with you sitting there than if we try to do it now. You can go get a drink somewhere when we're finished."

"Mother, may I?" Buck reached out and took the key. "You know, Muffin," he said, "you never disappoint. You frequently disapprove, but you never disappoint."

"That's one of the nicer things you've said to me."

"What can I say?" Buck replied, getting up from the table. "I'm in a gracious mood. Thanks for dinner."

CHAPTER EIGHT

She looked at her watch as she entered Restaurant Row and smiled seeing that it was six-thirty p.m. sharp. The text message was quite succinct, and she took great pride in following instructions to the letter. Her height gave her a slight advantage as she scanned the various signs hanging off the sides of the buildings.

"Would you like a seat, ma'am?" asked a maître d' from the doorway of the Mockingbird Café.

"No, thank you," she politely answered. "I'm looking for another address. Oh. It's right over there."

She pointed with a smile, walking across the alley and down two more cafés. She stopped in front of the wrought iron–gated patio of the PowWow Pub.

The door jangled, announcing her entrance. The outside lighting poured in through the large glass window, brightening the waiting area. She took off her sunglasses and approached the hostess stand. Behind the podium was a large, rectangular mirror. She glanced at her reflection while waiting to be greeted. Her blond hair was carefully pinned together, piled atop her head. Even in the dim lighting her natural lashes highlighted the insect blue–tinted contact lenses she wore in her feminine, almond-shaped eyes. Her tan was even and subtle, earned slowly, making her natural olive complexion glow.

A collegiate African American girl approached wearing a FSU Seminoles T-shirt, a pair of black pants, and a hostess name tag.

"Hi!" chirped the attractive and perky hostess, whose name badge read Andrea. "Just one, or will there be more joining?"

"Just one," the woman replied. The sepia-painted lips curved into a smile. "I have a patio reservation. The name is Barbe Truque."

Andrea glanced down over the reservation book resting on the podium, her face lighting up with a smile when she found the listing.

"If you'll follow me, please."

Andrea led the way through a bar crowded with college students all dressed in the colors of Florida State University. She stopped momentarily when the crowd suddenly burst into gleeful shouts of encouragement at the many television sets showing the football game.

"Sorry about the noise, but it's one of the first games of the season," Andrea said once they passed the bar and exited through a small doorway. "The 'Noles are playing the Gators. That's why we're wearing crimson and gold. You'll see it all over the city. It's a big thing!"

"To some," Mrs. Truque solemnly replied.

"You won't hear much out here," Andrea said, leading the way to the eight tables on the patio. Only half were occupied. "Most people are going to be inside watching the game, so you should have the patio almost to yourself."

"Good," Mrs. Truque solemnly answered. "I've never been much for American football."

"Well," Andrea answered, not knowing what else to say. "Your server will be with you shortly. Enjoy."

She grabbed the extra place setting and the Reserved sign before darting away.

Mrs. Barbe Truque folded her black skirt underneath her knees and sat down at the table. Two of the three tables in front of her were occupied, giving her the camouflage she desired. With only a slight extension of her long neck, she'd have an unobstructed view of the Mockingbird's entrance.

"Fifteen minutes to kill," she muttered. "Unless he's extremely punctual."

Knowing the odds, she chuckled at her own humor and perused the menu.

"Good evening," the handsome waiter said as he approached the table. He was wearing similar clothes to the hostess, except his crimson shirt presented the centered golden letters FSU. "My name is Jose and I'll be your server tonight. Can I get you started with something to drink?"

"Yes, please," Barbe said politely. "I'll have a lemon drop with Skyy vodka."

"Excellent," Jose confirmed, writing down the drink. "Are you ready to order?"

"The large Caesar salad with shrimp," Mrs. Truque answered. She folded the menu and handed it over.

"I'll be back in a few moments with your cocktail."

Jose walked off just as the sounds of *Pachelbel's Canon* rang. Barbe reached into her skirt's pocket and took out the phone with the lit-up screen. A cartoon cat holding a round clock showed it was not quite seven.

"Yes," she said. It was strictly an acknowledgment. "Yes, I am here. I'm betting he won't be here for another ten minutes. What? We'll see...oh. You are correct. I can see him coming down the alley now. Of course I'm sure. He's easy to recognize. Who else would wear such *gaily* colored clothes? I know what to do and how not to be spotted. Really? Because the last time I checked it didn't say 'stupid' on my forehead! I won't be seen. To be honest, I doubt he's that clever."

She slid her finger across the screen, ending the call, taking an extra moment to admire her well-crafted, manicured nails. Sliding down in her seat, crossing her legs at the ankle, she made herself comfortable. It was easy to see the single figure in a carrot-colored shirt and turquoise pair of pants. She watched him slow his pace, studying the addresses.

"Thank you, Jose," Barbe said. "When you get a chance, will you please bring the bill? I'm waiting for a call and will have to leave immediately afterward. Thank you."

When she looked up, Buck was disappearing into the Mockingbird Café. Making note of the time, she waited while the waiter returned with her food.

She put several bills inside before handing the check minder back to Jose, when he placed the large salad in front of her.

"Thank you," she said, reaching for her drink.

Mrs. Truque ate her dinner while keeping watch on the café's door.

❖

"Perfect timing."

Barbe Truque finished her drink as Buck came out of the restaurant, entering the alleyway. She stood to her full six-foot height and used it to navigate through the even more crowded television room, full of collegiate attendees and cheering Seminoles fans. Her rust-colored blouse was tucked neatly into the skirt, showing off her average-sized breasts and attractive figure.

From the safety of being inside, she scanned through the glass windows, searching for any glimpses of orange or blue. She caught sight of him passing by the last window.

Carefully sliding out the door, she let small groups of meandering people fill the gap between Buck and herself. She watched him turn the corner.

"*Un. Deux. Trois.*" She counted to ten before following. "With those colors, he couldn't have made it any easier if he was carrying a tour guide's flag."

She laughed to herself and continued through the crowd.

Another half block down he stopped suddenly to look at a window display.

"Shit!" Barbe muttered. "Sorry," she murmured to the person who slammed into her.

Moving out of the crowd, she stepped into a shoe store's doorway. Hugging the corner of the glass display, she peeked around.

She watched Buck check the license plate of a blue Honda Civic. Then she saw him get into it.

"I-M-A-D-I-K." Barbe repeated the license plate into her cell phone notes. "Now, that's funny."

After a few minutes she watched the car drive off.

Mrs. Truque left the arched door and began making her way back to Restaurant Row. She passed the alley and continued another block before finding her car.

Pachelbel's Canon sounded as she locked herself into the seat belt and turned on the engine.

"Yes," she said as she connected the Bluetooth system. "I just got back to my car. Don't be ridiculous. Of course he didn't see me. Give me some credit, this is not my first stakeout. There's no reason to be rude. Thanks, but I already got it. The license plate is a laugh riot! No. Let him think what he wants as long as he doesn't discover the truth. I know the address. Leave that to me. I'll take care of it when the time's right."

Mrs. Truque hung up the phone, shifted the dark green Miata into gear, and drove off in pursuit.

CHAPTER NINE

I'm curious," Buck said with a wicked grin, "if she's still there." Exiting the Mockingbird Café, he merged into the thickening crowds of the alley, slowly moving within its mass. Scanning the patio tables of the different restaurants, he noticed the different styles and cuisines offered. He slowed his pace walking down the alley but didn't stop.

Turning the corner, Buck browsed the store windows, checking the addresses as he walked. He stopped in front of a clothing store, noticing the mannequin's clothes as much as his own reflection and those passing by him. After another half block, he found Katarina's Cocktails & Burrito and the dark blue Civic parked in front. He walked around the car, smirking at the license plate.

"You couldn't have gotten me something a little more sporty?" Buck complained into the car's phone system. He was buckled in the driver's seat waiting for instructions.

"Didn't your mother ever warn you about judging things based on their appearances?" Muffin asked.

"Yeah, but I like you anyway," Buck replied. "Couldn't you have had the license plate saying I-M-A-G-O-D or something a little more accurate?"

"Give me a minute," Agent 69 said. "I'm tasting blood from biting my tongue too hard."

"Just tell me what it does," Buck said. He adjusted the volume of the Bluetooth speakers to keep his hands free. "I'm ready when you are."

"Turn on the engine."

Buck did as he was told. "Check."

"Turn on the radio," Muffin instructed. "It's programed to the Broadway station, so you should be very familiar with it."

"Very familiar," Buck confirmed. "But I hate that guy that hosts."

The beginning drumroll of "Everything's Coming Up Roses" roared out of the speakers. Patti LuPone's singing voice exploded forth.

"Now what?"

"Sing along," Muffin simply instructed.

Buck gave into the request. He got as far as the chorus before being interrupted by loud collective laughter.

"You are a gullible man, Agent 98!" Muffin said. His laughter changed into coughing. "There's a large group of us here and that was highly enjoyable. I may have to download that as my ringtone."

"Very funny, Muffin."

"Yes, it was," he confirmed. "Wasn't it?"

"Just tell me what the car does," Buck grumbled. "If anything besides annoy me."

"Turn off the radio and I'll tell you," Muffin said, his laughter subsiding. "Okay. The lever on the left of the steering wheel is for the wipers. Turning it away from you turns on the lights."

Buck followed the instructions.

"Now," Agent 69 continued. "Press the end of the lever with your fingertip twice in succession. If the lights flashed, you'll see the lit-up diagram of the car's outline on the dashboard."

"I see it," Buck confirmed. "It's in the bottom corner of the GPS screen."

"Once the outline is on, tap the button again and the red 'X' will appear next to one of the doors."

"It's next to the driver's door," Buck said impatiently. "Now what?"

"Hit the button to confirm and the X should changed to green. Once that's done you're set."

"Okay." Buck glanced into the rearview mirror again and smiled at what he saw. "What does it do?"

"It permanently turns off the seat belt in that seat only. It also gives special priority to everyone else except that seat. At least until the engine is cut, and then everything is reset to zero."

Agent 98 waited several moments in silence before asking. "And?"

"And what?"

"So it disengages the seat belt?" Buck asked, astonished. "Big deal. Does it also have an ejection seat that tosses him out of the car or something?"

"Nope," Agent 69 said. "This is real life, not a movie."

"Lame, Muffin," Buck said, disappointed. "That's just lame."

"One day you'll learn to trust my judgment, Agent 98."

"Well, it's not today," Buck said. "Remember how you were so sure that Mrs. Barbe Truque was just a friend of the family and not involved?"

"I remember saying it was *doubtful* she was involved. Why do you ask?"

"Because she's been following me since I left the café," Buck calmly reported. "I saw her walking away in the rearview when I first got into the car."

"Are you sure it was her?" Muffin asked. "You got a good look at her?"

"Not exactly," Buck said. "But from what I can tell in the photo I saw, the blurs match up. Besides, can you think of another reason why any other tall blond woman would be following me?"

"I don't know," Muffin answered. "Was she carrying a hit list?"

"Not even singing a show tune," Buck snapped back.

"Even though I can't see you right now, why do I have the feeling you're gloating?"

A car drove by, stopping at the light a few yards ahead.

"Muffin," Buck said. His tone changed to urgent. "I'm going to have to call you back."

Buck hung up the phone, dropping it into the empty passenger seat. Checking the rearview mirrors, he managed to pull into traffic just as the light changed. The black Jetta with the distinctive vanity plates reading HTCOCOA was only two cars ahead. He followed the car for another two blocks before it turned off and into a parking lot.

The well-lit sign facing the street of the Pilgrim's Church of the Holy Trinity stood in front as a sentinel for the filled parking lot behind it. Readable to anyone driving past the premises, the sign clearly stated:

TONIGHT'S DEBATE:
MARRIAGE EQUALITY—
THE ROAD TO DAMNATION
REV. C WALKER VS. PASTOR P. JACKSON

Buck twisted his head around to get a better view as he drove by the church. Finding parking a block up, he pulled in and turned off the engine. Getting out of the car, he made his way back to the church property.

"This should be interesting," Buck muttered.

The building appeared very square and boxlike as Buck approached, except for the twelve-foot-high looming cross jutting out from the steeple point over the door. Looking down with disdain upon all who entered, the ornament watched in silence as Buck entered the front double doors.

An elderly African American woman stood in the warmly lit foyer offering welcome to all those entering. Her face froze for a brief moment before changing into a forced smile.

"Welcome, my brother," the woman dressed in pink stuttered with surprise. Quickly catching herself, she smiled more sincerely. "Being new to our community, please feel free to browse over the pamphlets. If you'd like to talk to Reverend Walker, he will be staying later after tonight's debate."

"Thank you very much," Buck said. He took the offered brochure with the donation envelope paper-clipped to it.

Buck stepped into the chapel and looked over the rows of people seated in the pews. Slowly the conversation dulled to intense whispers, and Buck realized he stood out as the only Caucasian face present.

Looking around, he saw a black-robed figure practically flying down the aisle toward him.

"What in God's name are you doing here?" Phynilla ferociously hissed.

She took hold of his elbow with a plastered-on smile and forcibly began leading him toward the front door.

"Nice talk in the House of the Lord," Buck snapped back.

"I'm going to give you five seconds to leave," Phynilla offered. "Then you and I are going to have a major problem."

"Come on," Buck teased. He enjoyed the look of fear and discomfort fighting for dominance on Phynilla's face. "I think the subject is something I'd like to stay and listen to. I'm sure it will be very interesting. I don't knows nothin' about marriage equality, Miss Scarlett."

"You're going to turn around and get your lily-white ass gone with the wind, right now. Oh Kay?" She gave a quick look around to see if anyone was watching them. More and more curious glances were being thrown their way.

"Tsk tsk," Buck chided. "Look who's being racist now? Just what exactly are you preaching at this church of discrimination?"

"Listen, Buck." Phynilla's hand clutched onto his arm and her nails dug deeply into his biceps. "I'm not playing with you. You are treading on very thin ice and my nerves are worn even thinner! I have enough issues right now without you bringing anything new to the one place in life that is supposed to be sacred. Do *not* make me knock you down and snatch you back up baldheaded!"

"I'm not going to let this go," Buck promised. "I'll leave. But you and I are going to talk about it later."

"Without doubt!" Phynilla fiercely whispered. She offered a large fixed smile to a passing woman. "That's fine," she said with a more polite fixed smile. "You just go and let me explain why a gay white boy was coming in here."

"That's not fair," Buck said. "They can't tell I'm gay. I'm being subtle."

"You couldn't be more noticeable if you came skipping in singing 'The Best of Andrew Lloyd Webber.'"

"Got you there," Buck said, pulling his arm free of Phynilla's claw. "There's no such thing!"

He took a deep breath and ran a hand over his shirt to smooth it out.

"Sorry!" Buck announced loudly to Phynilla. "Wrong church! Good night."

Buck withdrew his wallet and took out twenty dollars, making a show of putting it into the donation envelope.

"A donation in your honor," Buck replied. He handed the envelope to the stunned elderly greeter in pink. "Thank you for your kindness. Others should learn from your example."

He flashed a snarky smile at Phynilla and went out the front.

Back in the car, Buck sat, listening to the sounds of his pounding heart. His hands hung on the steering wheel, letting his arms loosely drape off. The gears of his mind spun at high speeds, still getting nowhere.

"Maybe Muffin was right," he said, quieting his mind. "I need a drink."

Buck picked up his phone and scrolled through the notes he'd made on Tallahassee's nightlife. Disappointed if not astonished to see that no gay bars were listed within the capital city limits, he made note of the only listing of "gay friendly" he could find.

"El Savaje." Buck tried out the name and pulled into traffic. "It's better than nothing."

CHAPTER TEN

"Make the next right turn," instructed Osiris, the male voice from the GPS phone application. "Destination is ahead on the right."

Agent 98 slowed down more than necessary for the turn. Glancing in the rearview mirror, he was aware the car was still tailing him.

"Will you follow or not?" he asked the mirrored reflection.

The first two cars didn't. The small dark green sports car did. A SUV turned in afterward.

"Destination," Osiris declared.

Agent 98 ignored the announcement. Without slowing down, as if he were unaware of the address, he drove another block, purposely avoiding several available parking spaces. At the next light, Buck waited for the green turn arrow to change to yellow before making a speedy left turn. Immediately he turned into the 7-Eleven's parking lot, drove toward the back, and turned off his lights.

The small green car never made the turn. As soon as the light changed it continued forward. The red SUV behind turned, continuing down the street.

"Destination is behind you," Osiris reprimanded him. "Make a U-turn if possible."

"Shut up." Buck turned off the system. He remained still with the engine purring in idle. "Maybe I was wrong."

He pulled the car out of the lot and made a right at the light. After retreating back another two blocks he saw the small sign advertising El Savaje and turned in to the parking lot of Tallahassee's only answer to a gay bar. He pulled into the last stall in the sparsely filled lot behind the bar and parked. Prepping in the rearview mirror, he ran a hand through his chestnut hair, checked his perfectly even, white teeth, popped an Altoid, and made his way to the bar's entrance.

❖

"Here ya go, handsome. One lemon drop." The dark-haired bartender set a filled Cosmopolitan cocktail glass with a sugar rim in front of him.

"Thanks." Buck gave the man several bills, motioning for him to keep the change. Taking a sip of the drink he smacked his lips, turned his back to the bartender, and spun the bar stool around to take in the décor of El Savaje.

A handful of men filled extreme pockets in the dimly lit bar. Two men stood on the narrow catwalk that ran around the upper perimeter, gazing down at the small dance floor.

"Pretty much any bar USA," Buck concluded.

Spinning back around to face the bar, he looked up at the line of televisions that hung from the ceiling. They were all stationed to the same local channel with the volume muted to allow the sounds of the jukebox.

"Excuse me," Buck called out to the bartender. "What's that all about?"

"Oh, that," the bartender said, gazing up at the television screens.

Large groups of protesters were screaming and picketing in front of the camera crew. The footage panned over a long line of people shouting slogans and waving signs.

ADAM AND EVE—NOT ADAM AND STEVE!
IT'S SIMPLE MATH: 1 MAN + 1 WOMAN = MARRIAGE!

The bartender scoffed, waving his cloth at the screen. "That's that bitchy preacher man, Reverend Clarence Walker. He preaches at that church across town, the Pilgrim's Church of the Holy Trinity. It's mostly a black church. My mama's cousin goes there."

"I think I saw them getting ready this afternoon," Buck said.

"Looks like it they're at it again." The bartender pointed to the large gathering on the TV screens. "They're always shouting about gays going to hell or some shit like that. Honey, I say if all gays are going to hell, I'll bring the disco ball 'cause it's gonna be a party! Hey!" He snapped his fingers and continued with his duties.

Buck watched the reverend silently talk to a reporter. His actions were animated and the gathered group behind him showed their support without a doubt.

"Looks like they backed up traffic for quite a while," the bartender said. "That preacher man is always doin' some outrageous publicity stunt to draw attention to one of his causes."

"Is he always so…extreme?"

"Honey," the bartender said, putting his hand on his hip, "I think she doth protest way too much, if you get my meaning."

The bar door opened, allowing a sudden burst of light to penetrate the cavernous interior. A tall man stepped in wearing a dark blue button-down shirt and a well-fitted pair of black jeans. His dirty blond hair seemed naturally windblown like a surfer's as it fell down about his rounded face. All of the nine other patrons turned as one, looking up at the intruder, checking him out.

The man sauntered down the stairs as if in an old Western. He leaned across the Formica bar two stools away from Buck.

"A cold Redhook coming up, Benjamin." The bartender greeted the man before he could say a word.

"Thanks, Lee."

The man casually looked around the bar. When he saw Buck his teeth showed in a friendly grin, and he nodded politely. The bartender put the bottle in front of him and he took a sip.

"You know that Redhook got its start in Seattle?" Buck said. "That's where I'm from."

The man turned his head, studying Buck. His green eyes sparkled, catching the dimmest of bar light. He smiled, causing the trimmed darker mustache to crinkle over a set of white teeth with a small gap up front. Stubble cropped his jawline, covering his chin.

"That's where you live," the man corrected him.

"Yeah. That's where I live."

"I know where you live," the man continued. "I was correcting your speech."

"I didn't realize you were the Grammar Police," Buck said, taken aback. "I was only trying to make conversation, not narrate *A Game of Thrones*. Sorry to bother you."

The man couldn't help but smile. "Here's to Seattle," he said. Raising his bottle, he waited for his drink to be met.

Buck saluted back with a snarky smile, raising his drink and taking a sip without making the glasses touch. He immediately turned away.

"Come on," the beer drinker tried again. "Are you still jet-lagged or something?"

"How do you know I'm not from around here?" Buck said, turning his head and facing him with sparked curiosity. "And how did you know where I live?" The comment finally sank in.

The man's smile broadened in response. Sliding over to the space between them, he took a sip of the beer, making sure to keep his eyes locked on his newly found drinking bud.

"I don't hear even the slightest hint of a Southern drawl, and I can detect one at the lowest whisper. Plus you're wearing orange and blue—although that might be turquoise, it's hard to tell in this light. Either way, those are Gator colors. You're definitely ain't from around here."

"You just said 'ain't' and you're going to correct my grammar?"

The man's face lit up and he let out a hearty laugh that seemed to roll around the bar's perimeter.

"I had the feeling you were going to be sharp-witted, Mr. Miller," the man said as he was catching his breath. "I'm glad to see you didn't disappoint. Lee, can we get us another round here?"

Buck studied the man as he rocked his head back and polished off the beer. He put the empty on the bar as Lee replaced it, adding another lemon drop in front of Buck.

"Thanks, Benjamin," the bartender said with a wink at Buck.

"Okay," Buck said, taking a sip of his new drink and pushing away the finished one. "You know my name, and you say you know where I'm from...I mean, where I live."

"Seattle," Benjamin replied. "But you told me that."

"Then tell me something I didn't tell you," Buck baited.

"Ah." Benjamin closed his eyes as if trying to remember. "I can't recall your address but it has a four and a seven, but that could have been the number of the street instead of the house."

"Psychic or stalker?" Buck asked. "And should I be worried or amused?"

"I'd be flattered," Benjamin answered. "I don't memorize everyone's address when I get to check out their ID. Oh! I can see the wheels turning! He's at the ten yard line! He's at the nine yard line! The five and..."

Recognition finally dawned on Buck, and he snapped his fingers.

"You're the security guard at the governor's property."

"Touchdown!" Benjamin leaned over and clinked his bottle against the cocktail glass.

As he leaned forward Buck smelled one of his favorite colognes, Black Orchid.

"Sorry not to recognize you," he said. "But you had me at a disadvantage. I never saw your face."

"A boy's got to take whatever advantages he can get."

"Does that mean you get taken advantage of often?" Buck said with a salacious purr.

"Only when it's by my choice," Benjamin answered with a wink. "Let me officially introduce myself. I'm Benjamin Dover. If you become a good friend I may let you call me Benji, but that remains to be seen."

"Benji? Like the dog?"

"Just like the dog. I can be real nice when people rub my tummy. Or I can bite you in the ass." He growled playfully, snapping at the air, emphasizing his point.

"You've got to be kidding me."

"The nickname started as a kid. It's endearing, don't you think?"

"No," Buck said. "You're a gay man whose real name is Ben Dover?"

"How do you know I'm gay?"

"I'm calling it intuition." Buck gave him a deadpan look and one eyebrow arched.

"I swear," Benjamin muttered into his beer. "You sleep with one, maybe two hundred men and it gets you labeled."

"It's always the last fifty that seal the deal," Buck sarcastically informed him. "Mr. Ben Dover."

He gave a boyish smile, shrugging, knowing there was nothing to be done about his name. "Now you know why I go by Benjamin at work."

"Don't you get a lot of teasing about that?" Buck asked. "This is the South."

"Have you not met Phynilla?" Benjamin said with a wink. "Besides, I'm not really out at work, and those crackers won't think about putting it together."

"At least not to your face."

Buck shifted around until he and Benjamin were directly facing each other.

"How long have you been working for the governor?" Buck asked. Mentally he was taking notes.

"About six years. When he was first elected, my company was hired and they took volunteers. There were lots of guys that didn't want to work for a gay governor."

"How did he get elected, then?" Buck asked. "I mean no disrespect, but come on. He's a homosexual, Hispanic man in the southeast United States."

"I hear what you're not saying," Benjamin said, nodding. "Don't you remember the scandal?"

"You'll have to be more specific than that," Buck said with a smile.

"Remember Governor William Cox?" Benjamin explained. "He was that good ol' boy Republican guy who said he could trace his roots back to the fifth governor of Florida, the one during the Civil War."

"I didn't realize Florida was part of the Civil War," Buck confessed. "But I *loves* me a good scandal."

Benjamin's smile broadened. "Cox sent pictures of his homophone namesake to several political aides. Including one who was underage."

"It's coming back to me," Buck remembered. "Even with that, there were still several recounts before Governor Reyes was officially elected."

"That's true."

"Says a lot for the tolerance of the average Floridian," Buck said, not bothering to cover the contempt in his voice.

"Watch it, now," Benjamin said with a good-natured smile. "You're talking to a native."

"No offense meant. But you yourself said you couldn't be out at work."

"I said I wasn't out, not that I couldn't be," Benjamin

clarified. "But guilty as charged. They might know. They probably do but prefer not to mention it to me because ultimately, they don't want to know."

"I'm betting they have no problem over-sharing their lives."

"Bingo," Benjamin confirmed with a wink and a warm smile, showing off his white teeth.

The two men stared at each other, eyes locked together, the rest of their surroundings blurring and becoming nonexistent. Their breathing became one, sharing the air between them.

Benjamin rested his hand on the bar's edge. Buck set his drink down close by. The edges of their little fingers touched, igniting sparks.

"Out of curiosity," Benjamin asked, "do you like the theater?"

CHAPTER ELEVEN

Agent 98 looked at Benjamin with astonishment and slight skepticism.

"If you don't," Benjamin said, crestfallen, "it's okay. I know it's not everybody's thing. I know that not every gay man has to like theater. Nothing like being a stereotype, right? But I do. Like theater, that is. I like sports, too. There's no reason you can't like both."

"You really should make a beeping sound when you back up that fast," Buck said. He bit his bottom lip knowing it made him look boyishly cute. "If you give me a minute to answer you'll find out I happen to enjoy theater."

"Cool." Benjamin's seductive smile reappeared. He moved closer. "I was trying to figure out what to get Alejandro for his birthday next month."

"You mean Governor Reyes's son Alejandro?" Buck asked. His interest became distracted but remained steady on another level.

"Yeah," Benjamin said with complete nonchalance. "The kid is starting to develop an interest in musical theater. Miguel brought him to the Seminole Players' local production of *Company*. I was in it."

"Who did you play?" Buck asked. Benjamin's level of attraction was inflating.

The built blond sat up on his bar stool. He lifted his beer bottle and saluted. His biceps flexed tightly.

"Bobby."

"Bobby baby," Buck recited. "How long ago was that?"

"Six months ago," Benjamin said. "I think that's when he got bitten by the theater bug. Since then, I don't think that boy has missed a production, whether I was in it or not."

"Really." Buck folded his knees, resting his hands in his lap.

Benjamin counted off on his fingers as he recited.

"There's been *Phantom of the Opera*. I was Raoul. Then I played Riff in *West Side Story*. After that they did *Once Upon a Mattress*, and currently *RENT*. I wasn't in the last two productions. Alejandro wanted to try out for Jack in *Into the Woods*, but his father wouldn't let him. I try to make him copies of the CDs, so if you know your theater, what CD should I get him?"

"You don't know the various kinds of show queen wood you're giving me right now," Buck said with a smile.

"What if I say I have a signed picture of Sondheim at home?"

"Ding ding ding," Buck said excitedly. "And we have a winner. A round of drinks, please." He signaled Lee, the bartender.

"All that just for knowing my theater?" Benjamin asked.

"It's not as common an occurrence as you'd like to believe," Buck said with a wink. "And you lucked out. I happen to be one of the reigning show tune queens of the West Coast. If it's followed by 'Original Cast,' I own at least one version of it."

"And I was using the subject as a pick-up line. Who knew?" Benjamin commented. "So what would you recommend for the boy?"

Buck studied the handsome man and gave it thought for a moment.

"Find an illustrated copy of Joseph Moncure March's epic poem 'The Wild Party,'" Buck suggested. "Alejandro is what, fourteen years old? He's at the age where he'll start to understand it. Tie it in with either the Broadway or Off-Broadway cast albums. They came out the same year and both have excellent, recognizable names associated with them. Both have lyrics based on the original poem but different music written by separate composers."

Benjamin's smile widened, pulling him up to full height. His green eyes captured the dim bar lighting, letting them sparkle. "That's a great idea. Thanks."

"I told you I know my theater."

"Evidently. Between you and me?" Benjamin leaned in, lowering his voice. "I think the boy's just about to start the coming-out stages."

"Really?" Buck said. He was trying not to get lost in the scent of Black Orchid. "His father never mentioned it."

"Not sure if his father knows yet. Or Phynilla or Mrs. Truque." Benjamin shrugged. "The kid's been really cute asking subtle questions, making allusions to the subject and relating it all to his father."

"What did you tell him?" Buck asked, curious. "He's only fourteen."

"And how old were you when you knew?"

Buck thought a moment and conceded the point. "It's not like they haven't proven it to be hereditary."

"True," Benjamin said, acknowledging the possibility. "But it's usually passed through the mother's side, and there's no telling there."

"What happened to the boy's mother?" Buck asked, once again making mental notes.

"Died in childbirth," Benjamin replied. "Miguel told me."

"Miguel?" Buck asked. "Were you two, are you two involved?"

"No, I'm an employee of his," Benjamin said, shaking his head. "We were chatting one night and I told him I was gay, but that's all."

"Oh," Buck said. He failed in hiding his relief.

"I'm going to assume the same goes for you?"

"Oh." Buck crossed his heart and held up his hand. "We're

just friends. You mentioned that Truque woman. Why would Alejandro tell her? She's only there over the summer, isn't she?"

"They were very close," Benjamin said. "I thought they were related until Miguel told me differently."

"Truque?" Buck asked, trying to hide his interest. "Really?"

"Yeah," Benjamin said. "Alejandro doesn't connect with people that well. He was a shy kid."

"Was?" Buck said, pouncing on the word. "You said he *was* a shy kid."

"He was." Benjamin's smile was innocent, making him very attractive. "Whenever Truque is around him, Alejandro comes out of his shell. It would do him a world of good if she were there all the time."

"Why isn't she?" Buck asked, wondering just how much personal information this man knew.

"I don't know," Benjamin answered. "I think she lives somewhere else and only visits over the summer."

"Did the boy confide in you often?" Buck asked.

"Yeah, sometimes. He'd come over to the gate and hang out. We'd chat. Nice enough kid."

"Probably a first crush," Buck said. "I can see why."

He reached out, cupping Benjamin's jaw in his palm, his thumb seductively stroking the skin in front of the ear. The mustache spread over Benjamin's lips into an intimate smile.

"How long are you visiting the governor?" Benjamin shyly blundered.

"A little less than a week," Buck replied. "Why?"

"I was wondering if you'd like to have dinner on Sunday?"

"As in the day after tomorrow, Sunday?" Buck asked.

"Unless there's another?" He paused. "As long as you don't already have plans…"

"What? Oh no. No plans." Buck studied the handsome man sitting on the bar stool's edge, waiting with an anxious smile. There was little reason to resist. "Sounds good," he added.

Reaching into his wallet, he took out cash and a business card. Tossing a few bills on the counter for the bartender, he handed Benjamin the card.

Benjamin held the card up to his forehead without reading it. "'History Repeats Antiques,'" he recited. "'Buck Miller, sole proprietor.' That's all I remember except it's a California phone number. I did a Google search on you this evening on my break. I don't do well memorizing numbers."

"Then it's a good thing mine's on the card," Buck said. "And I moved to California about two years ago to open my business."

Benjamin looked at the card and smiled.

"That's my cell number, the phone I have with me." Buck paused. "Did you really look me up on the Internet?"

Benjamin blushed. Buck could see the crimson color creeping up his cheeks.

"Yes," he sheepishly confessed. "But I didn't stalk you here. This meeting is just coincidence, I swear it."

"A fortunate coincidence, then," Buck said.

"Yes," Benjamin agreed.

"It's been a long day, and I'm going to need my sleep to get rid of any remaining jet lag," Buck said. "How about walking me to my car. One hears so many stories about these tawdry Southern nights and the hooligans that prowl there."

Benjamin leaned over and let his palm quickly slide up Buck's leg before patting his thigh. "Now you know how those rumors get started."

The two men left the bar and climbed down the stairs heading back to the parking lot.

"Is it a good thing or a bad thing that Tallahassee has no listings for 'official' gay bars?" Buck asked. "Do you call that assimilation? Or is it a hint that some things in the South don't change?"

"I think having a gay governor says something," Benjamin protested. "Don't you? That has to show some progress. The fact that marriage equality is on the bill at all says a hell of a lot. If it passes, Florida would be the first of the Southern states to pass an all-inclusive law like that."

"Here's hoping!" Buck said as they reached the back parking lot.

"Which car is yours?" Benjamin asked.

"It's the last one," Buck said. He craned his neck to look for the Civic in the now-full lot. "Actually, it's the one behind that red SUV."

As they got closer to the back of the lot, Buck slowed his pace. His eyes were locked trying to think of why it looked familiar.

"This car isn't yours by chance, is it?"

Before an answer was given Buck was shoved forward, his face colliding with the doors of the SUV. Spinning around, he briefly saw Benjamin engaging in a fistfight with a person wearing a ski mask. Two other men, also wearing masks, were waiting for Buck with their fists up and ready.

"You okay, Benjamin?" Buck called out. He brought his fists up and bent his knees, ready to move.

"Holding my own!" Benjamin yelled back as his fist collided with the man's masked face.

"Then I guess that means you two and me." Buck challenged the men in front of him. "Two on one, eh? That takes me back to my twenties!"

The man to his right took a step forward and made the first swing. Buck ducked, grabbing hold of his arm. Using the shoulder as leverage he pulled the assailant directly into the SUV's doors. The man slammed into the vehicle and bounced backward, momentarily collapsing to the ground.

"What about you?" Buck turned his attention to the remaining man. "Let's go!"

"Fuck you, faggot," the man said through the knitted mask. He threw a test punch as if sparring in a boxing match. A couple of quick jabs followed but no contact.

"Did you *really* have to go there?" Buck said. He kept his back to the vehicle's doors, darting his head out of the way of the punches. "Now I'm going to have to kick your ass! Don't be a little girl. Throw a real punch."

The masked man bounced in place without attacking. Suddenly he lowered his head and charged full force. As he collided with Buck's stomach they were both thrown against the side of the SUV, knocking all breath from Buck's body. Rabbit punches were being delivered into his stomach and Buck could taste blood.

Wrapping his arms around the man's waist, Buck took hold and lifted him upside down. Taken off guard, the man stopped punching and tried to clutch Buck's legs. Buck threw the man to the ground and was pulled down on top of him.

"Ahh!" the man cried as he hit the pavement.

Agent 98 grabbed the front of his shirt and pulled the masked head off the pavement. Holding firm, he delivered punch after punch. Suddenly he felt a kick connecting to his shoulder and was thrown off the other man. He rolled backward, leaping up and readying himself for the oncoming attack.

"You okay?" Benjamin called out.

Buck looked over the shoulder of the men standing in front of him. Benjamin was coming toward them. The man attacking him was pulling himself up from the ground.

"I'm fine!" Buck called out, dodging a blow. "Look out behind you!"

Benjamin turned around but it was too late. The man's mask was torn off and Buck saw a man of stocky build and blond hair leaping forward, grabbing Benjamin by the waist. They fell to the ground, rolling across the pavement.

The short distraction was all his attackers needed. The two remaining assailants rushed Buck and all three men crashed to the pavement. Buck managed to roll out from underneath the pile. One man was already on his feet. The other was trying to get a clear shot in.

"Ahh!" Benjamin let out a pained cry.

Buck looked over to see Benjamin's body convulsing on the ground. The blond man stood over him with a Taser in his hand, trying to catch his breath. He looked up to see Buck and smiled maliciously. Picking up Benjamin's shirt collar, the blond threw a straight punch and knocked Benjamin out. The body shook on the ground before stopping.

"Oh shit," Buck muttered. "That's not good."

He rolled away only to find someone grabbing hold of his ankle. Buck tried to turn over and his leg was roughly shoved aside. The masked man threw himself on top of Buck, trying to pin him down. They bowled across the pavement, hitting up against car tires. Picking up his head from the pavement, Buck slammed his forehead into the man holding him down. The force of the blow sent the man reeling backward and off him. Buck scrambled up and jumped onto the man's chest. Using his knees, he pinned the man down by his shoulders.

"It may not start off that way," Buck said, throwing another fist into the man's jaw, "but I always end up on top!"

"Not always, you fucking Gator faggot!"

Buck felt a foot plant itself squarely between his shoulder blades. He was thrown by the kick and smashed into the side of a car. Two hands pulled him up by the shoulders. In a moment he was flying through the air and colliding with the blue doors of a van. His breath was knocked from his lungs. Slowly sliding to the pavement, Buck tried to catch his breath. Blood, sweat, and pavement scrapings blurred his vision, and he tasted more blood on his tongue and lips.

The blond man sauntered over. The smug, triumphant look on his dirtied face was drawn close. He kneeled, looking directly into Buck's eyes.

"Fuck you!" He spat in Buck's face, watching Benjamin convulsing from the Taser's electric shock. Taking hold of Buck's carrot-colored shirt, he delivered the knockout blow.

CHAPTER TWELVE

Phynilla Jackson let the last congregation member out of the church and locked the doors behind them. She looked at her watch, not realizing it was so close to midnight, and was amazed that the debate had gone on as long as it had. The entire church seemed to have turned out for this, and that at least was a good thing. Showing their passion regardless of the debate's outcome.

With her back to the front door she looked down the red carpeting to the empty pews, amazed that less than an hour ago, these halls were filled with shouting and arguments, Bible quotes and readings of Holy Scriptures. She looked up at the cross hanging over the centerpiece altar, silently contemplating the differences between faith and duty.

Phynilla let out a heavy sigh and started down the aisle. No longer dressed in the robes of a pastor, she held the position's uniform folded neatly under her arm. At the end of the carpet, she hesitated before the door leading to the reverend's office. She knew he was there, but her fist froze in midair several times before she finally committed to knocking.

"Reverend," Phynilla said. She slowly opened the door, pressing her body against the broad side. "Reverend, I think we need to talk."

The Reverend Clarence Walker sat behind his desk looking very handsome in a sky-blue pullover and a pair of khaki pants.

The small rectangular glasses he wore reflected the light as he looked up from his papers. A smaller man by nature, he appeared an imposing figure sitting at the desk with his sermon notes and Bible open before him. Seeing Phynilla standing there, he placed his pen next to the legal pad on his desk, folding his hands in front of him.

"Come in, Pastor," he said softly. "My door is always open."

"I don't mean to bother you if you're working on your sermon," she said. Hesitantly she slid into one of the two empty chairs on the opposite side of his desk.

"No bother," he said. "I'm working on the front sign for this weekend's message."

Phynilla looked at the desk. Even upside down she could easily read the words:

> *God destroyed Sodom*
> *For their sins*
> *Let Him not our country too.*

"See," Phynilla said slowly as if it caused her pain, "this is exactly what I want to talk to you about," She folded her hands on the edge of the desk. "Why is that sign necessary?"

"Because the sinners of the world have made it so."

"Why can't you leave their judgment to God, and you can worry about more important matters?" Phynilla asked.

"What is more important than the laws of God?" Reverend Walker asked.

"Nothing if you were the person to uphold them, but this is a man's world and we follow man's laws. You're spending so much time and energy on something that is inevitable," Phynilla argued. "Why can't you just accept that this is the right thing to do?"

"Because it isn't!" he snapped. Closing his eyes, he took a breath and calmed down. "The Scriptures are very clear on this matter. 'He who lies with a man—'"

"Yes, I am very aware of that particular Leviticus passage." Phynilla cut him off. "I was at the debate, in case you didn't see me."

"How could I not?" Reverend Walker solemnly replied. "You were on the opposing side of God."

"Now watch your mouth, Oh Kay?" Phynilla said. She pointed a long finger with a French manicure at him. "I have never been on the opposing side of God, but your will and God's are not always simpatico."

Reverend Clarence Walker stared at her from across the desk. His face was tight, resembling a pug's, and his jaw remained locked.

"What you want me to do is inconceivable," Reverend Walker said. "We are a violent society, allowing all too much debauchery and vice to prevail in our country. If we don't take a stand against sin, we are going down the same road as the emperors in ancient Rome."

"I think that's a little extreme, don't you?" Phynilla asked.

"Not at all," Reverend Walker said. "If we don't stop this sin, it will spread."

"And what about what you're doing?" Phynilla asked. "What about the hate you're begetting in the world? I'd be careful, your house has a lot of glass windows."

"When it comes to God's laws," Reverend Walker said, "there is only right and wrong. I know I am right."

"And I know you are wrong."

Reverend Clarence Walker took a breath and fully sat up in his chair. "How can doing God's will be wrong?"

"Because you are doing it at the expense of others," Phynilla said. "Marriage equality is going to happen. It's a matter of time. It's already spread out from the random state to over a third of our country. Why can't you do as the Bible says, hate the sin but love the sinner? The Scriptures are clear. 'Give the command and the persecuted shall be free.'"

"It is beyond that now," Clarence said shortly. "We are

engaged in a holy war and I will not stand aside and watch the Bible be trodden under our feet."

"I heard all this during the debate," Phynilla said with a heavy sigh. She shifted in the chair. "Why can't you be contented to preach to your congregation and leave the rest of it out there? These people love you, but they aren't going to follow you blindly into a political swampland. It's not fair, or right, or even Christian to try and influence how they vote in private on any subject."

"It is my job as the Lord's shepherd to keep any of His flock from straying into a wolf's den."

"Try treating them as people instead of sheep and see how much further you get with them."

"I don't think I need advice from you on the subject," Reverend Walker said. "Especially not from one who is employed by the enemy."

"As I've told you many times before," Phynilla said. She closed her eyes for a moment, taking a deep breath, trying to keep calm. "My career, my private life, and my personal devotion to God, I keep all separated from one another."

"That's not a talent all of us can claim." Reverend Walker looked down to his notes and picked up his pen. "Some might even say you were a slave to your job."

"Now ain't that the slave calling the kettle black!" Phynilla sat erect in her chair. Her eyes were wide with anger and her nostrils flared with heavy breath. "I think I need to go home. I want you to know I'll be praying for you!"

The chair scratched across the floor as she pushed back and stood up. Turning to the door, she stopped when Clarence called out.

"There is one more thing."

Phynilla froze at the doorway. Slowly turning to face him, she stared coldly, waiting for the axe to fall.

Reverend Walker smiled when he realized how long he could keep her waiting in an anxiety-filled silence.

"I need to ask for your resignation as pastor."

Phynilla stared at the man with the tiny gloat on his face, refusing to show him any satisfactory reaction. "I can't say it's unexpected."

"If you can't support me and you can't support our church," he said, "then you have no business here." Reverend Walker went back to his papers.

"The Scripture is very clear," he said without looking up. "Galatians tells us that if you follow the desires of sinful nature, which include sexual immorality, lustful pleasures, and impurity, then you will *not* inherit the kingdom of God."

"And Romans says that everyone has sinned; that we all fall short of God's standards. I think that includes you."

"I'd think about your own actions before picking up that stone."

"I know where I've been," Phynilla answered. "I have no doubt of His forgiveness. Can you say the same?"

"I think it is time you left." Reverend Walker stood up from the desk, leaning over it menacingly and challenging Phynilla with a cold stare.

"Is this your idea of being a true Christian?"

"Being a true Christian is one thing," he said. "Betrayal by my sister is something I cannot forgive."

"I'm going to leave," Phynilla said, standing as she slowly spoke, trying to keep her temper under control. "You will have my resignation as pastor on your desk tomorrow, and I won't say a word about anything once I leave. But I know things about you that you think only God knows, and neither of us is very happy with you right now."

"I'm not so concerned with you," Clarence said. "If there is a problem, I'm sure the Lord will let me know."

"As the saying goes," Phynilla said, "your arms are too short to box with God."

"That remains to be seen." He went back to his work.

Phynilla left the room without waiting to be dismissed. Closing the door behind her, she removed her hand from the knob before it started to shake with anger. Turning around, she retreated down the carpeted aisle at a quick pace. Before leaving the chapel, she looked back at the altar, up at the beauty of the wooden pulpit and the cross that was mounted behind.

"Thank you," she whispered.

There was a moment of surprise when she realized there was no anger behind her words. Then there was a flood of relief.

CHAPTER THIRTEEN

Buck opened his eyes to find his face being pelted by raindrops. A slivered moon allowed beams of light to break through the shadows of tree branches with beards of Spanish moss. The sharp shards of water sent renewed pain to his head. Every nerve in his body seemed to be inflamed and every muscle was heavy and spent.

"Buck. Can you hear me?" Someone was calling his name. "Buck!"

"I hear you," he muttered, trying to sound coherent. A deep breath eased the pounding in his head. "My entire body aches. Where the hell are we?"

"Listen to me," Benjamin instructed sternly. "You need to pull yourself up and get your legs out of the water. Now."

"What?" Buck's head was foggy. He propped himself up on his elbows.

His legs were submerged from the knee down in the swampy water. Two nearby logs floated half-submerged, with fallen moss and twigs mixing with the film on the water's surface.

"My legs are tied to something," Buck said. "I need to pry them loose."

He looked around and started to lean toward the log floating five yards away.

"Buck," Benjamin yelled. "Don't move."

Freezing in mid-motion, Buck looked over his shoulder and

saw Benjamin pushing himself upright. He looked filthy with dried blood and mud caked on his face and clothes.

"Listen to me," Benjamin commanded. "You need to pull your legs out of the water. Now! That's not a log. That's an alligator."

Buck looked back to where his arm was still extended toward the approaching log. It was then he noticed the two bark-covered knots were a set of cold, staring eyes. The edge of the log rose into the air, shattering the illusion and letting the twigs float through its widening mouth.

"Oh my God," Buck exclaimed.

Agent 98 spun over and dug his hands into the muddy bank. Taking handfuls of dirt with him, he clawed his way out of the water.

"It's got my legs," he yelled, feeling a resistance from both sides. "Help!"

Benjamin reached down, grabbing hold of Buck's wrists. Stepping back, he pulled until Buck's legs were out of the water. Large pieces of pink meat were tied to the lower part of each leg.

"I can feel it biting my legs," Buck yelled.

Benjamin pulled him farther up onto the shoreline. He lost his footing and slipped backward, pulling Buck on top of him. Agent 98 landed facedown in the mud-covered crotch of Benjamin's pants.

"Not the way I wanted to end up here," Buck said. He lifted his head with an attempted smile, the dried mud cracking on his face. "But I'm not one to complain about the good results."

Benjamin sat up, meeting Buck face-to-face. He stared into his hazel eyes and returned the smile in force.

"You look like a hot survivor of a zombie apocalypse."

Reaching out, he took hold of the back of Buck's neck, pulling him close. Their lips touched. The excitement of the danger locked them together. Slowly, both mouths opened to receive, and their kiss became deeply passionate.

"I feel like I'm in a Tennessee Williams play," Buck said, breaking their kiss. His breathing was hard, coming short and fast. "Am I a goner?"

"Not yet, Blanche," Benjamin said. "It's these wet ropes that are biting into your legs. We should get them untied. Then we need to find a way home."

"No arguments here," Buck said. He rolled off Benjamin, propping himself up by the elbows. "Why in the world would someone tie a ham to my legs?"

"Because of the gators," Benjamin explained, as if this were an everyday occurrence. His fingers puzzled with the wet rope, trying to get it untied.

"Watch." Benjamin stood up and tossed the pork into the water. The log floating nearby sank subtly below the surface.

"And that thing was how close to eating my legs?"

"Probably wouldn't have happened. Gators don't usually like dead food to be handed to them. But why push it?" Benjamin leaned down, offering Buck a hand up. The two men were quickly pressing together. Benjamin stood a few inches taller and he wrapped his muscled arms around Buck's waist.

"I'm not dead yet," Buck answered in a Monty Python accent.

"That's why your legs were in the water," Benjamin continued explaining. "They don't usually attack anything bigger than themselves. Gators prefer to sneak up on prey and pull them under for a death roll. Generally speaking, they are lazy creatures and won't normally go for anything they can't eat in one snap."

"Hello!" Buck said. "It did snap at me."

"No," Benjamin said. "It opened its mouth to hiss. That's just a warning. We're probably near a nest or something."

"You're not making me feel any better."

"How's this?" Benjamin leaned in and they kissed. It was gentle and soft, letting their lips enjoy the heat shared and rising between them.

"Better," Buck confessed. "Let's get out of here before the crocs decides to come back."

"Alligator. Crocodiles aren't native to the U.S.," Benjamin corrected him. "And I hate to tell you this, but we're surrounded by them. I'm guessing for a while now. Those aren't bullfrogs you're hearing."

Buck's head snapped around as he looked in every direction and listened to the sounds of alligators croaking.

"Holy shit. They're everywhere!"

"Calm down," Benjamin said with a laugh. "I've lived here all my life. Really, they aren't going to attack unless provoked."

"Shouldn't we get out of here in a serpentine way?" Buck asked. His hand demonstrated with a zigzag motion. "I've heard gators can only turn on right angles."

"Come on," Benjamin said. He reached out, taking Buck's hand. Searching for a pathway, he led them away from the water. "That's just a myth. Besides, there are worse things out here than gators. There are far better chances of spider, snake, or scorpion attacks than gators biting a human." He paused, looking up, pointing. "There are a few bats right there."

"Really! Not helping," Buck said. He squeezed Benjamin's hand until he cried out. "Why in the hell would someone do this to us?"

"This was a warning for something. I have no clue as to what." Benjamin continued, "Most likely it was just a college prank."

"Really?" Buck said with astonished disbelief. "Did you get a good look at that blond guy? He's a little too old for collegiate pranks. I'm thinking gay bashing. We were attacked in the parking lot of a bar. Maybe something else even more sinister?" He didn't explain any further. "Why in the world would anyone play such a deadly prank on a stranger?"

"Melodramatic much?" Benjamin said with a laugh. "You *are* wearing orange and blue, Gator colors."

"For the last time," Buck said with disdain, "the pants are *turquoise*. And it doesn't matter now because they are the color of mud and aren't getting clean. If this is a joke, it's not funny. Aren't these people civilized?"

"People take football very seriously here in the South. In some circles it's as strongly revered as religion. And that's not something you want to cross here in the South."

"That's because they'll *burn* a cross here in the South," Buck spat back. "I got these clothes in Rome and now they're ruined."

"Get over it," Benjamin said with a laugh and a squeeze of his hand. "It's just mud on some clothes. It's not the end of the world."

"Excuse me, Croc—I mean, *Alligator* Dundee," Buck said playfully. "I didn't grow up wrasslin' with gators. Some of us enjoy the more sophisticated aspects of life."

The dirt path led out of the trees, intersecting with a one-lane paved road with small mushroom-shaped footlights every few yards. Benjamin stopped to look in each direction.

"This way," he said, nudging his head to the right. "I think I've figured out where we are."

"Are you going to tell me? Or is this a guessing game?" Buck asked. "Because so far I'm thinking…outer layer of hell?"

He slapped his arm, killing the mosquito that bit him.

"Not even close," Benjamin replied.

They continued down the paved road until another path crossed their way. Planted in the corner was a signpost. A small yellowing bulb dimly lit up a wooden sign of a bat, its wings pointing the way to the Bat Cave or the Main Gate.

"Wakulla Springs!" Benjamin announced.

"Doesn't help."

Benjamin gave Buck's hand another playful squeeze. His hand felt nestled in the meaty palm.

"We're about fifteen miles south of Tallahassee," Benjamin explained, pointing off in the distance. "Every kid in the area has made a school field trip out here at one point or another. Lake Swan would be another fifteen miles in that direction." He pointed opposite.

"So what do we do now?" Buck asked. "I'm not looking forward to walking fifteen miles back."

"I'm guessing you don't have a cell phone on you either."

"Left it in the car," Buck answered. "I try not to take them into bars with me—it ruins the pant line."

"We'll find a pay phone," Benjamin said, ignoring the comment.

"What is this thing you speak of," Buck responded. "A pay phone?"

"Very funny."

"I'll tell you one thing," Buck said. "My first day in Florida really sucks!"

"I'm not sure how to take that."

The men followed the path and came to the Welcome Center.

"I can't believe you actually found a pay phone," Buck said snidely. "If that doesn't prove that the South is still behind the times, nothing does."

Benjamin rolled his eyes as he told the operator the number for the collect call.

"Just be thankful they still have these talky wire contraptions," he replied. "Otherwise it would be a long walk. Hey, Clayton, it's Benji. Sorry to call you so late, but I have a big favor to ask…"

Chapter Fourteen

T hat will be one I won't be living down for a while," Benjamin said.

He put the key into the lock of the second-floor apartment and opened the door for Buck to enter.

"Not only is it just three a.m. now," he continued, closing the door and turning on the main light, "but picking me up in the national park, covered in mud, with you, is going to give him fodder to ride my ass for a long time."

"Touch of envy," Buck muttered with a wicked grin. "Tell him you picked me up and I have a mud-wrestling fetish."

"That's one way to explain it," he answered. "I don't have many other options. When he calls later, I'll have had time to conceive a plausible story."

Benjamin leaned against the door, pulling off his shoes. "Excuse me a minute." He walked off to turn on the bathroom light.

Buck looked around the apartment. He moved around the glass coffee table and blue cloth couch, making a beeline for the two large bookshelves stretching from floor to ceiling.

"Right now," Benjamin called out, "my body hurts and I want a hot shower. Then I need to climb into bed. I have to work at ten a.m."

"It's Saturday," Buck said, aghast. He glanced over the titles of the books. "Is being governor that dangerous a position that you work on weekends?"

"I guess it is when you're a gay one," Benjamin called back. The sound of a toilet flushing was heard as he walked back into the room. "I'm with a private company. We're hired to be there from nine in the morning to six at night every day except for Saturday and Sunday, when we go in at ten. The shifts alternate like any other job. Are you looking for something to read?"

"I always find that someone's bookshelf will tell me more about a person than what's said."

Buck scanned over the books by Victor Hugo, Alexander Dumas, Leroux, and Proust. His fingertip traced the spine of a thick Parisian travel guide before taking a French-to-English dictionary off the shelf.

"I'm guessing Francophile." He opened the dictionary and scanned over the pages.

"I've always wanted to go to Paris," Benjamin said with a yawn. "But have no idea when I'm going to get the chance. All I ever do is work. Until I make it there, at least I can read about it. If you're looking up dirty words they aren't in the book."

"What the hell?" Buck muttered. Distracted by the entry he read, he flipped through until finding another. "But if that's true, then now what?"

"Buck?"

"Sorry," Agent 98 muttered. He put the book back on the shelf. "Believe it or not, that just helped me figure something out…"

Buck stopped in mid-sentence, turning around. Words completely failed him. He stood wide-eyed, with his mouth hanging open, delighted.

Benjamin unbuttoned his shirt at a tantalizing, slow pace as Buck watched. Each one undone allowed the shirt to pull open a bit farther, revealing an outlined set of pectoral muscles covered with a thin coating of dark blond hair. Perfectly man-scaped, the hair was trimmed to the meeting of the collarbone, where it stopped completely. The shirt was pulled back and off, tossed to the floor like a mechanic's towel. Buck saw the hair stretching across the broad chest toward the shoulders and disappearing under the thick set of arms. The biceps and triceps were well worked, looking like a flesh figure eight turned on its side, connecting the shoulder to the elbow and on to the wrist. The blond traces made their way downward, creeping over stenciled abdominal muscles, dissected by a darker patch running above and below the navel. The trail enticingly vanished into the belted waistband of his pants.

"Your car is only a block or two away and I'm happy to take you back if you want," Benjamin said. His fingers moved lower, manipulating his belt buckle. The muddied pants fell and he stepped out of them. "But that would mean I would have to get dressed."

Buck allowed his eyes to rise past the pair of formerly white socks that Benjamin wore. His strong calves gave way to a solid set of thighs. The muscular legs reached upward, disappearing into a snug-fitting pair of forest green rectangular trunks with a black waistband. He couldn't help but notice the swelling flesh pressing against the inside of the underwear, his and Benjamin's respectfully.

Buck walked over with a cocky attitude and smile to match. Keeping focus on Benjamin's green eyes and reaching down, he cupped the cloth-covered bulge in his right hand.

"God forbid I should be inconsiderate," he whispered. "Especially to such a gracious host."

The two men listened to the sounds of their mutual quiet breathing, staring into each other's eyes reflecting desire. They leaned in, letting their lips touch. Buck ignored the gentle scratching of Benjamin's mustache, moving past the burn to the pleasure of his kiss. Their lips parted and his tongue invaded like a warring crusader to the eventual inevitable, willing surrender.

Buck's arms reached under Benjamin's as his hands massaged the muscles of his back, gently moving downward until his palms slid over the thin layer of cloth covering the round curves of Benjamin's buttocks. His middle fingers traced the subtle crevice between the firm cheeks, and his thumbs gently massaged the tailbone invitingly pointing downward.

Benjamin growled low and guttural. He pushed his hips firmly against Buck's waist. The passion increased as their lips parted only long enough for Benjamin to pull the orange shirt over Buck's head, revealing a defined swimmer's build with a carefully trimmed dusting of dark chest hair. He slid his palms downward over Buck's chest, cupping each pectoral muscle and giving the nipples a gentle tweaking with his thumb and forefingers.

Buck closed his eyes and opened his mouth with a low, pleasurable moan. Benjamin slid forward and covered Buck's mouth with his lips, his tongue flickering and teasing as they pulled each other closer. Benjamin's strong fingers slid around Buck's hips to the belt buckle up front. The men remained locked at the lips, hungrily exploring each other, as he expertly unlocked Buck's trousers. The muddy clothes fell to the floor followed by two sets of shucked-off underwear.

"We," Benjamin said after several short pants, "we should get in the shower."

"Lead on, McButt," Buck said. He playfully slapped Benjamin's ass cheek. The sharp sound echoed in the silence.

"Follow me." Benjamin kissed him and led the way.

Buck watched closely as he walked to the back of the apartment.

"With an ass like that, how could I not?"

CHAPTER FIFTEEN

W hat's wrong?" Buck asked. He put the car into park and, using the electronic panel, lowered the driver's window. The light drizzle decorated the windshield with droplets.

Benjamin's black pickup truck remained idling on the side of the road. The driver's side door was ajar and smoke puffed out of the exhaust.

"The turnoff to Lake Swan is the next left," Benjamin said. He bent down and leaned in the window of Buck's car. "Follow the road and you should come to the gate." He glanced at his watch. "I'm guessing Jimmy will be there by now. He's the one who was with me yesterday. I'm going to wait here and let you go on in first. I'll give you a call later about tomorrow."

"What's the big deal?"

Benjamin's jaw tightened and his lips almost disappeared. A low, discouraging growl rumbled from his throat.

"It's bad enough that you're coming back in the same clothes as last night, only muddier," Benjamin said with an uneasy grin. "But if we came back together, that would just be a little too easy for even those guys to figure out. Remember I'm not out at work."

"Look at it this way." Buck winked. "It'll be so much easier to come out if you go in with me."

"That might be the problem. I don't feel the need to come out at work. If they find out, they find out. But I don't need to flaunt it in front of them."

"How is that flaunting?" Buck looked at him with an incredulous stare. "Have any of them ever brought their dates or spouses to work? Have you met any of their wives?"

"Which are you?" Benjamin asked. "A date, a spouse, or a wife? At this point I'd have to say none of the above."

Benjamin reached through the window and ran his hand along Buck's arm. "Look," he said softly. He looked behind them to make sure no other cars were coming. "I had a really fun time last night *and* this morning, swamp and all. You're a sweet guy, but I can't take the chance of going through that gate with you and letting them have that over me. Sorry, but that's the way it has to be."

"Oh I get it," Buck said. "You can suck my cock but can't drive into work with me. No, it's cool, I understand."

"Come on, Buck. That's not fair. There's a big difference between being a gay security guard in the South and being a gay antique dealer in California."

"You're right," Buck said. "I don't have to pretend to be something I'm not."

He flicked the button, forcing the window to rise, pushing Benjamin away. The car moved about three yards before he pushed the brake pedal. After glancing in the rearview and seeing Benjamin remaining still, Buck put the car into reverse.

The security guard bent down to the window as it lowered.

"Hey," Buck sharply said. "I'm not happy about this, but I'm just visiting and you live here. We can discuss it tomorrow over dinner."

Benjamin glanced about for any others present. He leaned into the window and kissed him. "I think we can find better things to talk about." Benjamin withdrew and stood up, taking a step away from the car. "That is if we have to talk at all."

"I'll wait for your call," Buck said. "Don't keep me waiting too long. You're not off the hook yet, I don't care how cute you look!"

"How about if I get us tickets for something?"

"Oooh, tickets," Buck said. "That'll work. I love tickets. And I've been wanting to see something for a while; it's gotten good reviews, I hear."

Placing the car into gear, he drove off to make the first left turn. Within a mile he came to the locked gate across the roadway. A sign that said "Private" hung in the middle over the mesh. Buck slowed the car, bringing it to a halt as the stout security guard sauntered over.

"Good morning, Jimmy," Buck said.

The guard bent down his round frame to look into the car window. "What's your business?" Again the drawling voice. "You got an ID, boy?"

Buck rolled his eyes, fishing the card from his wallet.

"You do know we went through all this yesterday?" Buck handed over the plastic card. "I'm a friend of the governor's? I came in yesterday afternoon with Phynilla? Does any of this ring a bell? Hello?"

The guard studied the card and looked at Buck with a diligent fish eye. He grunted and handed the card back. Before Buck could take it he let go, and the ID fell onto Buck's lap.

"Gimme a minute," the guard said with a surly attitude. "I'll get the gay."

"Excuse me?"

"Gate," the guard replied. "I said I'd get the gate. Don't get your undies in a bunch."

"Tell me," Buck said with a fixed snide smile, "when did you lose your passion for your job?"

Jimmy sneered as Buck rolled up the window. The car pulled through after the gate was opened and Buck waved politely to say "thank you" as he passed.

Parking the car in the roundabout, he noticed only the Town Car in the drive.

"Thank goodness," Buck muttered as he got out. He stretched in the morning sunlight and started off toward the house. "If Phynilla were here I'd be sure never to hear the end of it."

Buck made it around the corner before he heard the alarm sounding. "Oh shit!"

The sounds of the three dogs barking rolled down the hill like an avalanche. He stood still as they approached, leaping up through the grass, Jenny's knitted rabbit ears flopping as she alerted all within earshot, with the Earle and the Marquise barking right behind.

A quick shrill whistle and the dogs immediately silenced. They trotted back to their mistress.

"Well," the countess said. She lowered the rifle as Buck approached. "Don't you look like hell on a biscuit?"

"Thank you," he replied. "And good morning to you."

"Too much fun or too much trouble?" she asked with a grin. "Or should I not ask?"

"Some from column A," Buck answered. "Some from columns B and C. Take your pick."

"Come on, young man," she said with a twitch of her head. "You can get cleaned up and I'll make you breakfast. It's Saturday, so outside of Miguel, no one should be here for another hour or so. And my nephew won't be up for a while yet. No one has to know but us."

"Thank you," Buck sincerely said as they made their way to the house. The three dogs trotted alongside them as if escorting a prisoner to the execution wall. "How does Miguel come to have such a young aunt?"

"I was Mother's surprise," she said, clutching Buck's arm and giving it a squeeze. "I'm only fifteen years older than my nephew. Maybe that's why he's always been special to me."

"You know," he said with great appreciation, "You're an okay lady."

"I'm a lot wiser to ways of the world than people give me credit for," she said. "Our country seems to discredit anyone over sixty years as being old and feeble. I've learned to use it to my advantage. That's why I spend so much time abroad. That and I love to travel."

"I think a broad is a good way to describe you."

"You got that right," she said, winking at the doorway. "You go clean up. I'll meet you in the kitchen."

❖

Buck entered the bright room to the smells of fresh coffee and baking waffle. He appeared cleaned and dressed casually in a pair of fitted blue jeans and a plum-colored T-shirt that clung to his chest. Sitting at the small table, he looked out the window, seeing the grassy hill out front. A plate of waffles was put down as the countess took her seat opposite.

"Countess," Buck said through the first forkful.

"Please," she said, patting his hand. She took a sip of coffee. "Call me Margareta. It's so much simpler. Everyone here bothers with such formalities, and honestly, I'm over it."

Margareta smiled, allowing a natural grace to shine across her face. Her hair was perfectly styled, parted slightly off center and brushed up off her forehead. The crafted arches of the brows and the playfully irreverent blue of her eyes let a mischievous twinkle subtly nest within. The simple line of pearls around her neck spoke of her modesty.

"Okay," he said with a warm smile. "Margareta. What exactly is your deal? There's not much that surprises me. You took me completely off guard yesterday. How is that?"

"Oh that," she said as if answering a question of fact. "That was my second husband, Robert Stewart. He was a wealthy English gentleman who insisted I learn the basic techniques of defense. He said it was the duty of every Englishwoman to learn to fight for Elizabeth and Country."

"You've been married three times?" Buck asked.

"That's correct, dear." She pointed to her left hand and the three wedding rings she wore. "I was a rebellious girl and ran away to Europe. My family disowned me until I met and married Count Nicholas Valois from Nice. But by then I'd already said, 'The hell with you,' and I haven't spoken to any of them ever again. Except for my nephew."

She paused for a breath, her eyes glazing over with memory. She smiled impishly over the edge of her coffee mug. "I loved him very much and he was a beautiful man. Charming, handsome, and good in bed. When I lost him I was devastated. The only thing he left me was the title of countess. And wonderful memories."

"I'm sorry."

"Don't be," she said. Blinking several times, she came out of her memory and smiled, giving his arm a pat. She pointed to the next ring. "The money came with Robert. It made his loss much easier to deal with."

"And I'm guessing that big diamond is from your third?"

"Yes, my dear husband Zelig Rosenblatt."

"Where is Zelig now?" Buck asked. He finished the waffle and pushed the plate aside.

"I think," Margareta said, taking a moment, "he and his boyfriend Lamar are in Budapest right now. Oh, but I do love the shocked expression when I say that to people."

"Again," Buck confided with an admiring shake of his head, "I'm not usually surprised by much."

"Zelig comes from an Old World Orthodox family of jewelers. I'm not having children, so I can afford to give him the cover he needs. And he gives me the jewelry I desire. It's a perfect marriage."

"I don't mean to be rude," Buck asked. "But how is that a marriage?"

"My dear boy," she replied. "Now you've shocked me. Of all my relationships, I can't tell you which has given me a better life. People like to talk of 'traditional marriage,' but that's all I ever had. Marriages of love, of money, or convenience have been going on since the beginning of time. Newsflash! They always will. That's why I came back to lend Miguel my support during all this R-65 nonsense. To be honest, my gay friends' marriages are the only ones that seem to last anymore."

"Forgive me if I change my mind," Buck said. "You're no broad. You're a true lady."

"Thank you," she said with a wink. "Still, I'd rather be recognized as the latter, but known better as the former."

Margareta's expression fell in a flash, her eyes widening and smile fading to two lips flat-lining. She craned her neck to look past Buck and out the window.

"I'm not sure what this is about," the countess hesitantly said. "But it can't be good."

Buck spun around in his chair to see Phynilla storming her way up to the front door.

"This isn't you," Buck said. "This is about me."

"Then I'm going to leave you to it." Margareta stood up, bringing her dishes to the sink. "Before she gets in here, I need to ask a personal favor."

Buck's head snapped up. Margareta stood still, her expression stoic.

"Bring Alejandro home safely. He's my grandnephew and I love him dearly."

"You know?" Buck whispered in shock. "Everyone here has been so careful not to let you find anything out."

"Never underestimate an older woman, Mr. Miller." She cut him off with a wink. "Plus thin walls, and I'm an accomplished eavesdropper."

"Why not tell them you know?"

"Why give them something else to worry about?" she answered smartly. "Plus, I do love the pampering they give me, thinking I'm old and feeble."

"You're an incredible woman, Margareta."

"I know."

"You are such an A-hole!" Phynilla yelled at Buck upon entering the room.

"On that note," Margareta said, "I think I'll take my leave."

"I'm sorry, Countess," Phynilla replied in a saccharine tone. "Excuse me, I was just leaving. Good day," she said to Phynilla. She gave a quick nod to Buck. "Good luck."

Phynilla's eyes were wide and sharply alert as they followed the countess from the room. As soon as she was sure Margareta was out of earshot, she snapped around to Buck. The coffee cup jumped as her palms slapped down on the table.

"You and I," she leaned over until her face was inches away from his, "we need to have a talk, Oh Kay!"

CHAPTER SIXTEEN

"We can talk," Buck said. "But you're going to have to get out of my face first. It's far too early for ugly."

"Maybe you should have thought about that before ambushing me last night!"

Buck rolled his eyes, taking a sip before speaking. "Don't be so melodramatic. I didn't ambush you, I just went to church."

"Think that's funny, do you?" Phynilla's eyes were wide with anger. Her lips practically disappeared as she clenched her jaw. "You're the one who followed me. Don't think you were that sly that I didn't see you two cars behind."

"Hey," Buck said. He snapped up and sat full in the chair. "I didn't plan on following you. You drove by me, Ms. Hot Cocoa, and I admit it, I was curious as to where you were going."

"And you had the audacity to follow me into my church?" She punctuated the last few words by pounding on the table.

"Forgive me if I'm wrong," Buck said, picking up the mug to avoid spilling. "But the last time I checked, churches were open to the public."

"So you decided to start your search for God in that particular one?" Her nostrils flared. Dark circles held up each eye socket.

"With such a welcome sign out front," Buck hissed back. "What did it say? 'Marriage Equality—the road to damnation!' And when I saw your *name* on the roster as pastor! How could I not go in?"

"You don't have a damn clue about the hot mess you are about to step into."

"Well then," Buck forcefully said. "Tell me how a black woman in the South can be so friggin' hypocritical when it comes to the equality of others!"

Phynilla stared at Buck for a long moment. Her eyes grew wider and her breathing became audible. Her hands snapped to the sides of her head. "That's it! Somebody hold my earrings, I'm going to kick your ass!"

"What the hell is going on here?" Miguel came into the kitchen dressed casually in a pair of Dockers and an emerald-colored pullover. His vision volleyed between the two others. After seeing him they retreated to silent seething.

"We can discuss this another time," Buck suggested.

"I ain't got no secrets!" came Phynilla's sharp reply. "We can discuss this now. What the hell was you doing causing trouble at my church?"

Miguel's eyebrows rose with surprise and he cast a questioning look at Buck.

"Okay," Buck said. He took the last sip of his coffee. Sighing loudly, he looked between Miguel and Phynilla, finally resting his gaze on the governor. "I followed Phynilla into her church last night," he confessed. "I wasn't trying to cause any trouble. I was just curious when I saw her name on the sign up front."

"Why in the world would you go to the Pilgrim's Church of the Holy Trinity?" Miguel looked at Buck with complete surprise. "It's devoutly pious, no offense, Phynilla, and the congregation is mostly African American. You don't really fit in on either account."

Phynilla folded her arms, rotating her head on her shoulders. Her bronzed lips puckered, bringing a sanctimonious expression to her face.

"You don't mind that she's pastor at an anti-gay church?" Buck asked.

"Why would he?" Phynilla answered. "Until today, I've had no reason to bring my personal spiritual beliefs into my workplace!"

"Come on," Buck said. "You don't see a conflict of interest?" Phynilla was about to reply when Miguel put up his hand.

"I've known since she first came to work with me about her connection to the Pilgrim's Church. I had her checked out," Miguel explained. "Her professionalism spoke for her, as it should, and it's never been a conflict at my office or anywhere else, for that matter. She's been a great asset to me, so why would I care where she goes to church? And no offense, Buck, but I don't owe you any explanation for whom I hire."

"I guess my question is for you," Buck said to Phynilla. "Why would you be a pastor of a church when the reverend is so vocally outspoken against homosexuals?"

"Because," said Phynilla with a snide edge to her voice, "the Reverend Clarence Walker is my brother."

"You've got to be kidding me" was Buck's stunned response.

"No. I'm not. He's my brother, and he's a damn good preacher!" Phynilla said. "He's had the gift since he was a young boy. He's always made good use of it and would have a wonderful future in front of him if he'd only get off his soapbox about gay marriage."

"Yeah, if only," Buck replied. Sarcasm dripped from each word. "Don't you think it's ironic that he's so outspoken against gay marriage in Florida, when twenty years ago interracial marriages were illegal, and fifty years ago he was barely considered a citizen?"

"I said my brother was a good preacher," Phynilla said defensively. "I didn't say he was a good man. There's a very large difference, and the two can be separated out."

"Even so, it's one minority attacking another," Buck said. "Whatever happened to hate the sin and love the sinner?"

"The African American community is a very spiritual one,"

Phynilla said with a little more calm entering her voice. "It's very deeply rooted in religion. It dates back to slavery days and..."

"Oh, you want to play the oppression card?" Buck cut her off. "How did your mother take it when you told her you were black?"

"Mother took it well," Phynilla said in an edgy tone. "It was quite the surprise for dear old Dad!"

Buck stared back into her deadpan expression. The edge of his mouth began to twitch its way into a smile. He started to laugh. The other two quickly joined.

"Laughter is a good mediator. I think we should all take a deep breath here," Miguel suggested, taking his own advice. "I knew Phynilla was going to be involved in the debate last night. She was taking the opposite side and arguing for the church to accept marriage equality. She was trying to help get R-65 a little more accepted in the community. We've previously talked a great deal about how to get a little more enlightenment brought in."

"Really?" Buck said, astonished. He glanced at Phynilla, who was simultaneously glaring and gloating.

"I was trying to explain that marriage equality is not only the right thing," Phynilla said calmly, "but it's also an inevitable one."

"Really?" Buck repeated.

"Every legal adult should have the same legal right. It's not our place to pass a moral verdict on what they do privately. I tried to explain that we need to vote for what's fair, and leave the judgment to God."

"How did the debate go?" Miguel asked.

Phynilla cut him a sharp look and took a deep breath. She closed her eyes for an instant and opened them as she exhaled.

"I'm not sure," Phynilla honestly said. "There was a lot to say last night. We didn't end until midnight. Then the reverend and I spoke for quite a while afterward."

"What did he have to say?" Buck asked.

Phynilla looked at him with a tight expression. Her jaw was

set and she sucked in her cheeks. After studying him quietly for several moments she answered.

"That's between me and the reverend," she stated calmly. "And God."

"The question that begs to be asked now," Buck said, knowing he was pushing the mood of the room. His eyes sparkled mischievously. "Do *you* think gay people *should* be allowed to marry?"

"You don't need to answer that, Phynilla." The governor intervened before she could speak.

"No," she answered. "It's all right. I don't mind. The honest truth is that I'm often torn on the subject. There's a lot I disagree with when it comes to the homosexual community."

"Things like equality. Fairness. Justice," Buck said. "Or are you going to quote me Leviticus again?"

"The Bible is clear in what is written…"

"Oh that!" Buck scoffed. "A book written by many men over the course of hundreds of years that consistently goes against the natural law, teaching oppression and prejudice."

"Now watch your mouth before I smack it closed," Phynilla said. She put one hand on her hip. "You don't need to blaspheme around me. If you let me finish for a change, you might have heard me say that I also believe that every human being should have the same equal rights. We are talking man's laws here, not God's. I will vote for marriage equality because it is the right thing to do. Any other opinions are strictly between God and myself. Oh Kay?"

Miguel put his hand between her shoulders and gave her an affectionate pat. Beethoven's Fifth Symphony rang out from his pant pocket. Walking to the far end of the kitchen, he reached for the phone.

"I'm sure you and God have a lot to talk about," Buck said to Phynilla.

"You know, you might want to give it a shot," Phynilla responded. "It probably wouldn't hurt you to get to know God."

"I know God. I like God," Buck said with a smile. He waved his hand from his head to his waist. "Obviously God likes me, too. I mean, look at all this."

"As Proverbs says: 'A man's pride will bring him low, but a humble spirit will obtain honor.'" She offered a tight smile. "I guess we know which fits you."

"Hello?" Miguel said into the phone.

The momentary pause was shattered by the governor's hoarse cry.

"*M'ijito*? Are you okay?"

CHAPTER SEVENTEEN

Alejandro turned his head upon hearing the heavy door dragging open. Two voices entered, arguing, bringing with them fresh air and a warm breeze from the outside. He was certain he recognized one of them.

"You go soft on me now and I'll kill you right here," said the first voice. "Brother-in-law or not, I'll put a bullet through your head."

Alejandro wasn't able to recognize that voice; it was the other one that had the accent. He heard the door being pushed shut and smelled the dust clouds that were stirred up.

"I'm not going soft!" The second voice. "There's something about this new guy that's visiting. I get a bad feeling from him."

"The antique dealer you called me about all in a panic?" the deeper, rough voice mocked with a laugh. "He's nothing to worry about. I already took care of that."

"What do you mean?"

"Two of the boys and me met up with him and his boyfriend last night. I doubt either one gives us any more trouble. Gators will eat anything, even a couple of faggots."

"Looks like one of them got a good shot on you," said the familiar voice.

"Lucky punch," shouted the other. "I'll have a shiner for a few days. Believe me, he's worse off for it, so fuck you!"

Alejandro's wrists were hurting from the plastic ties binding them behind his back. He flexed his fingers, scraping them against the rough wall of stone that he was pushed up against. A sharp edge scratched the tip, catching on the plastic before letting it pass over.

"No," the familiar one shouted back. "Fuck you! Fuck us all! Don't you think something happening to a visiting friend of the governor's might raise some suspicion?"

Alejandro became more alert at the mention of his father, but had no idea who else they were talking about.

"Nobody's talking to the police, not as long as we have him."

Heavy footsteps approached. The boy twisted his body, trying to guess what was happening. The restraints cut into his small chest and thighs where they tied him to the folding chair.

Without warning a strong backhand crashed into the side of his head. The blow sent him slamming sideways into the wall, the rough stone cutting his cheek. Alejandro whimpered and cried into the duct tape covering his mouth.

"Shut up or I'll give you something to cry about," the voice shouted down at him. "This is what happens when faggots have kids. They're brought up to be wimps and sissies." He cried mockingly back at Alejandro. "Shut up and be a man!"

A strong push rocked him back into the wall. The man stepped away from him.

"Dude. Chill out," the familiar one said. "He's a kid."

"My sister never did anything so stupid as to marry you," the other snapped back. "And I'd never have hired you if she weren't pregnant. I don't know which of my brothers-in-law is stupider, but you don't see him in here whining at me. No, he does what he's told! What do you think's going to happen?"

An uncomfortable silence briefly settled.

"R-65 gets vetoed," came the slow stuttering answer. "And we let the kid go somewhere?"

"You are so fucking stupid!"

There was a shuffling of objects and Alejandro heard a heavy clicking sound. He let out a muffled yell as something shot by his bare foot, hitting the dirt floor with a heavy thud. Instinctively he moved his feet, the only movable part on his body besides his head, wrapping his ankles around the backs of the chair's legs.

"The next one goes through his throat. What did you think was going to happen?"

"I don't need this kid's blood on my hands."

"Pull your head out of your ass," hissed the angry one. "Who chloroformed the kid? Who took him off the property? Your hands are already covered in his blood."

"I told you I would help protest R-65," the other snarled back. "I never signed on to kill any kids!"

"I never signed on to have a country where a nigger is president and a spic rules the state. The stripes on the Florida flag are red, not pink. It's time we put the white back into the White House."

"None of that has to do with the kid."

"The last sacred thing in this world is the word of God," he said. "Marriage is meant for one woman and one man. Only! We let fags marry and they have kids like this. It has everything to do with him."

Alejandro kept his breathing under control.

Keep yourself cool and calm. His father had taught him that. *Stay calm and the answers will present themselves.*

But this wasn't a school exam!

Alejandro listened to the conversation, trying to recognize the other voice. His fingers traced the roughness until they once again found the sharp edge barely sticking out of the wall. It was a twisted nail's head. Bringing his arms up behind him, he slowly worked against it.

"What the hell do you think you're doing?"

The boy froze.

"I'm giving the kid a drink of water."

He allowed himself to breathe again. Someone was coming toward him. It was a slower step, calmer than before.

"He hasn't eaten in a day and must be hungry."

Alejandro tried to speak up. The tape muffled his words. A strong hand was put on his shoulder. It remained still, holding him firm.

"I'm going to take the tape off," the man said. "I'm going to give you water from a bottle. If you scream, I'm going to let my friend shoot a nail right into you. Do you understand me?"

The boy nodded.

"*Esto va a dañar,*" he warned. "On the count of three."

Alejandro felt a hand touch his face and scrape an edge of the duct tape. Getting a grip between his fingers, the man counted in Spanish before ripping it off. A moment later the hand moved to the back of his neck and the lip of a plastic bottle was held to his lips.

"Here you go."

His head was tilted back and the bottle poured water into his mouth. Greedily he swallowed gulps until his head was tilted back upright. The bottle was taken away.

"*Gracias, Angeleno,*" Alejandro whispered, finally recognizing the voice. He panted heavily.

When there was no response, Alejandro began to think he might have been wrong.

"*Todo estará bien,*" was the reply, after another long moment's silence.

"For Christ's sake," the other man shouted. "You're in America! Speak the language if you're gonna live here."

"I'm going to give you a banana," the man said to him.

Alejandro felt the soft fruit held to his lips. He bit at it ravenously, devouring it in a few short bites.

"Now that's rich," snarled the other voice. "Look at how naturally he eats it. His father must have taught him that."

"Enough of that," said the closer man. "What do you want me to do?"

"Here's what I'm going to do. Let me in there!" An excited malice crept into the snarling voice. A cabinet door opened and was slammed shut. "We're going to give Daddy another call.

Maybe while they're chatting away in Spanish, I'll put a nail through the kid's foot. That should get the point across."

The man stomped over to the boy and grabbed hold of his ankle. Pulling it out from under the chair, he forced it flat on the dirt ground. Alejandro stopped struggling when he felt the cold edge of a gun placed against the top of his foot.

"Are you going to do what I say?" the man yelled at the boy. "Are you?"

Alejandro nodded, whimpering.

"You better do exactly what I say, or so help me God, I'll put a hole in your foot like Holy Jesus. You understand me, boy?"

Alejandro bit his lip to keep it from trembling. He nodded, his breath rattling audibly in his throat.

"Open the bag and hand me the phone," the man commanded. "Did you download the app like I told you?"

A plastic bag rattled.

"Here," the other man said. "It's downloaded."

"Good, read me the number from the table."

After he read each number, Alejandro heard an electronic chirp.

"Now you got ten seconds to talk. You do anything funny and I'll fire this gun right through your foot. Understand?"

Alejandro nodded. A plastic phone was roughly held against his ear.

The phone sounded with a long, dull ringing. It echoed in the cell phone's shell. A longer silence followed. The low rolling sounded again, and abruptly ended as someone answered the other line.

"Hello?" The governor's voice crept into Alejandro's ear.

"Papi," he whimpered. "It's me."

"M'ijito." His father's frantic reply. "Are you okay?"

"I'm all right. I'm just scared," Alejandro said. "I miss you, *Papi.*"

"Alex," his father said. "You'll be home soon. I promise. You can count the minutes."

"I have been," Alejandro said in an oddly calm voice. "I'm up to 535,600 minutes." He forced a chuckle through the phone. There was a beat of silence before Miguel's confused response.

"We'll have many seasons of love. Don't worry, *m'ijito.*"

The phone was pulled away from Alejandro's ear. A few beeping tones were heard as a new application was put into use.

"Alejandro? Alejandro!" Miguel's panicked cries came distantly through the phone speaker.

"You're running out of time!" the man said into the phone.

"You hurt my son and I'll find and kill you!"

"Kill R-65 or we kill your son. Time's running out. Tick tock, Governor. Tick tock."

The phone chirped off.

"Now," the man at Alejandro's feet said. "That should get him going."

"What do we do now, wait?" said the other.

Alejandro felt the gun being put down next to his foot. The grip on his ankle was released.

"Hand me that roll of tape. I need to gag the boy."

The man used both hands to reapply the duct tape to Alejandro's mouth. He stood up and walked away.

"*We* don't do anything," he said. "*You* take this phone and get rid of it."

"What do I do with it?"

"Throw it in a Dumpster. Toss it in the water. Shove it up your ass for all I care. You just need to take it and get the hell out of here now, before the call is traced."

Alejandro's foot found the nail gun. He placed his foot on top of it.

"We're finishing the job today."

"Perfect. Take it with you and get rid of it."

"Why can't you do it?"

"I need to finish my work here. Don't just stand there! Get your ass and that damn phone outta here!"

The door slid open and pulled shut with a slam. Alejandro heard no other sounds for several long minutes. When he was fairly certain the men weren't coming back, he moved his foot from under the chair. Slowly, he moved his other foot and carefully slid the nail gun underneath him. Both feet returned flat on the ground in front.

Alejandro's fingers crept over the wall behind him. He located the nail and continued his task of carefully picking away at the restraints. Letting his fear fuel his determination, he rhythmically sawed away. A song came to his mind and he worked with the music in his head. The clear, powerful voice of Idina Menzel urged him on, and like her iconic character from *WICKED*, he was determined to Defy Gravity.

Chapter Eighteen

Y ou hurt my son and I'll find and kill you!" Miguel shouted into the phone. "Alejandro?"

The caller had disconnected.

"Give me the phone," Buck commanded.

Miguel immediately tossed it over to him. Buck began pressing buttons, activating the codes at once.

"They'll call me as soon as they can trace it," Buck said. "Phynilla, get him some paper. Governor, you need to write down everything that was said."

Everyone scrambled to their assigned tasks. A thick silence settled in the room. Audra McDonald's rendition of "My Stupid Mouth" rang out of Buck's phone. In a flash he held it to his ear.

"Please tell me you have something," Buck said. "Okay. Is it still there? At least that's good news. That...not so much. Do what you can. What?" His expression changed into a pout. Miguel handed him the transcribed conversation. "Fine. Send me the address and I'll be there."

Buck clicked off the phone to see the others staring at him.

"At least we have some good news," Agent 98 said. "We know Alejandro's alive. That's the best news we can get. How did he sound?"

"Frightened, but I don't think he's been hurt," Miguel answered.

"Right there. Good news."

"He sounded calm," Miguel said. "You don't think he was drugged, do you?"

"If he sounded coherent and what he was saying made sense," Buck suggested, "I'd doubt he was drugged."

Miguel spun around and paced through the kitchen.

"The next thing is the phone call came from within the Tallahassee city limits. Since this is the second time, we can assume that if the kidnappers are still in the vicinity, then so is Alejandro."

"Thank God," Phynilla said.

"We have a much better chance of finding him if he's kept local," Buck said. "Now we just have to find him."

"Are you any closer?" Miguel said.

"We're narrowing it down."

"How?" Miguel demanded. "How are you narrowing it down? What kind of progress have you made since you've been here?"

"Considering I've been here less than twenty-four hours," Buck was trying to keep calm, "I think we're on course. I understand you're frantic, but now's not the time to turn on me."

"On course?" Miguel's voice rose two octaves. "I don't care what's on course, I want my son back!"

"We're doing everything we can," Buck said. "But I need you to stay as calm as possible. Let's focus on what we know. Alejandro hasn't been hurt, and you know he's alive. We know that he's more than likely somewhere in the city limits."

"That's not good enough," Miguel yelled. Heavy tension crashed in front of them. "I want my son back! If he's not back here by Monday, I have no other choice but to start the veto process. My son is more important to me than my right to get married."

"No one would blame you if that's what you need to do," Phynilla assured him. She put a reassuring hand on his shoulder, glaring at Buck.

"No. No one would. But I promise it won't be necessary," Buck said quietly. He looked over the paper in his hand. "What's all this about seasons of love?"

"It's from the musical *RENT*," Miguel replied. His staunch stance softened.

"Yeah," Buck said with a sarcastic chuckle. "I know."

"Alejandro played that CD over and over again. He was always singing the songs."

"I think I must have heard him play it at least 525,600 times," Phynilla added. "And that was before he went to see it."

"When was that?" Buck asked.

"Last weekend," Miguel answered. "He begged me for tickets but I couldn't go. I sent him with Mrs. Truque. What's so funny?"

"Nothing," Buck said. "Mrs. Truque intrigues me. You'll be happy to know that I don't think she's involved with the kidnapping."

"I tried to tell you," Phynilla said before the governor did.

"You'll have to excuse me," Governor Reyes said. "I'm going to grab a cup of coffee and start writing a draft to veto R-65."

"Governor…" Buck protested.

"I'm giving you as much hope as I can," Miguel explained. "The reality is I'm the governor of Florida, and I need to be prepared."

"Don't do anything hastily," Buck said. "We still have time."

"I'm going to make the announcement that I'm vetoing the bill at tomorrow's rally."

"You don't need to do that, Governor," Buck said. "Give me a few more days. It's been less than twenty-four hours. They're counting on you emotionally caving in."

"I can't handle this!" Miguel said. He was on the verge of tears. "You can't imagine what's it doing to me."

"No," Buck said softly. "I can't. Listen to me. If I can't find him and get him back by Thursday, I'll be the first one to say veto the bill. But give me more than twenty-four hours to bring Alejandro home. Don't kill the bill tomorrow. Let the rally inspire you further. Let it remind you of all the work that still needs to be done."

"I hate to say it," Phynilla said. She folded her arms across his chest. "He's right."

Silence took over for several long moments. Miguel nodded, conceding.

"I need to ask you," Buck said. "Can you think of anyone in your past who might want to cause you or your family harm?"

"I'm the first openly gay governor of a Southern state," Miguel said. "I've had threats and insults hurled at me since day one."

"Do any stand out?" Buck desperately asked. "Anything in particular at all?"

Miguel stood still with a cup of coffee in his hand. His eyes slowly moved back and forth as he stood, contemplating the issue.

"There was a guy a few years back," Miguel finally said. "He made several calls to my office making threats to kidnap and kill me."

"And you're just telling me this now?" Buck exploded. "Don't you think that might have had some relevance to this?"

"No, I didn't!" Miguel snapped back. "It happened over ten years ago when I first started my political career. The calls were traced to a phone booth and a man was charged. The calls stopped as soon as he was picked up, and they never started again."

"What happened to this guy?" Buck asked.

Miguel stopped to think. "He said he didn't do it and was interrogated but released due to a lack of evidence."

"Do you remember his name at least?" Buck said. He was highly irritated.

"Peter something," Phynilla said. "His first name was Peter."

"Peter Sarto," Miguel recalled. "But there was something about him that made me think he didn't do it."

"I'll look into Mr. Sarto," Buck said. He wrote the name down. "And I'll be the judge of that."

"Excuse me," Miguel said. "But I have work I need to do."

Phynilla and Buck watched him shuffle across the kitchen, a broken man. His head hung low and shoulders were rounded forward with defeat. His left arm hung listlessly by his side. He left the room in silence.

Phynilla flew across the small table until she was nose-to-nose with Buck.

"If you don't find that kid and bring him home safely," she hissed, "I swear to Holy Jesus that you'll be hitting those high notes, and my cat will have a new set of balls to chase under the couch. Oh Kay?"

She stood up, glaring down at him. Buck slowly pulled himself to his full height, then leaned forward, his hands braced on the edge of the table.

"First of all," he said slowly, "I have an excellent success rate." He paused, giving a quick mental review. "Yeah, I do. Second, I don't like threats. Especially not when it comes to my goodie bag! So I will ask you to take a step back and let me do my job."

Phynilla's breathing could be heard across the table. She kept her eyes locked with his, fighting with herself to keep control.

"You damn well better know what you're doing," she resigned herself to saying. "You damn well better."

"It would have helped if someone had told me about Mr. Sarto before this."

"As the governor said," Phynilla reiterated, "the man was released due to lack of evidence."

"That doesn't mean he didn't do it," Buck snapped back.

"The man used that phone booth to call his pregnant wife," Phynilla said. "If I remember correctly…"

"And I'm sure you do," Buck instantly replied out of habit.

"The man's story all checked out," Phynilla continued. "He worked in that area and called his wife on his breaks."

"No one found this odd that he used a pay phone instead of an office phone?" Buck asked. "And that it just happened to have come from the same phone the threats came from?"

"People are innocent until proven guilty," Phynilla said.

"Tell that to O.J. Simpson," Buck snapped.

"Oh no you did *not!*" Phynilla warned. "Do *not* get me started on O.J.!"

Her stare continued to bore into him as she turned to leave the room.

Buck felt his cell phone vibrate in his pocket. Taking it out, he checked the text message.

"Really, Muffin?" Buck moaned. "A pretzel stand at a flea market?"

CHAPTER NINETEEN

"Well," Buck said, making the most of the situation. He watched the endless masses roaming through the entranceway. "At least I feel pretty and thin."

Buck joined the crowds at the open flea market, bemoaning the fact he had to be there. As one of the last drivers directed into the parking lot, he'd found it difficult to find an empty space. Once the spot was taken, the attendants moved to a different lot, leaving the area vacant. The lined-up cars stretched on silently like the condemned at prison roll call—large trucks and compact cars as far as the eye could see. It wasn't until he moved from the lot and around the closed machine repair shop that he saw the flea market and the throngs of people herding their way inside. Stretching over the vast fairground, the front entrance opened to an ant's nest of serpentine rows winding back on one another before leading to another mile of parking.

Browsing the endless rows of stalls, he began the task of looking for the Twisted Pretzel stand. Secluded in the third row, between Bella's Twilight Trinkets and a funnel cake stand, Buck saw the hanging banner with a skull shaped out of pretzel dough.

"Nice stand," Buck said, approaching the stall.

A tall redheaded vendor stood behind the counter. A heated glass case with pretzels in the shapes of daggers, skulls, bombs, and pistols hung on a rotating rack within.

"Are you Buck Miller?" said the vendor in a thick Scottish brogue.

The burly, bearded man was dressed the part in plaid kilt, a matching sash over a white shirt, and a sporran hung prominently in front of his crotch.

"Yeah," Buck said, taken aback. Looking the man over from head to toe caused his lips to curl into a hopeful smile. "Have we met?"

"No," the heavy brogue croaked out. The Scotsman gave him a careful look, taking in the snug-fitting blue jeans and chest-clinging, dark purple T-shirt. "Let's just say you were described to me."

He reached into the heated display case with a set of tongs and withdrew a pretzel shaped like a dagger. After dipping it into a small cup of dark brown mustard, he handed both over to Buck.

"I was told to give this to the man fittin' your description." The "R"s rolled seductively. "And the lass paid me well, I might add."

Buck stared at him with surprise, almost dropping the small cup of sauce. "Did you say a woman paid you?"

"Aye, I did." He glanced over Buck once more. "I'm guessing a good friend of yours?"

"That depends," Buck said. He took a big bite of pretzel as he scanned the crowds around him. "What did she look like?"

"Quite the looker she was," the vender stated. "Tall, tan, and blond. Nice figure. She didn't leave a name. Nor her number." He winked with a large smile.

"Thanks," Buck said. He threw a five-dollar bill into the tip jar. "I appreciate your help."

Turning his back to the pretzel stand, Buck let his eyes scan over the clusters. People passed in all directions, crowding the winding walkways. Buck started off, continuing farther into the warren of stalls and stands. His vision was well trained to scan the basics of human features, much like the focus on a highly developed camera.

Staring back at him from the end of the row stood a tall woman with blond hair pulled back from her face. She was wearing a pair of sunglasses with large rounded lenses covering her eyes.

Buck stopped in the middle of the row. The human stream of people diverged around him like a stream around a rock. He locked eyes with her before she turned and darted away into the crowd.

"Game on, Mrs. Truque," Buck said. He licked the last of the mustard from his lips with renewed excitement.

Agent 98 took off, pushing his way through the crowd as best as he could. As he turned the corner he scanned the rows for any glimpse of the particular blond shade of her hair. He saw her standing to the side just inside an open tent stall for alligator jerky.

She peeked out from the stand and saw that he was following. Trying to hide her height, she darted off into the center stream of people.

Buck continued to make his way through. When he turned the corner to another row of crowded stalls, he momentarily lost sight of her. Darting between two stands, he cut his way into the center of the next winding row. Facing the oncoming people, he quickly scanned over them and saw the pinewood blond hair and sunglasses coming toward him.

For the briefest of moments she didn't see him ahead of her. Suddenly she stopped. Her reddened lips rounded perfectly in complete surprise. She spun around and worked her way against the crowd like a salmon swimming upstream.

"I love it when they run," Buck said, accepting the challenge.

His blood pumped and he felt an electrical charge running through his body. He watched her cut between several of the stalls before taking off in hot pursuit.

She moved quickly, slicing her way through the crowds. Buck followed with the same ease. Mrs. Truque weaved deeper into the flea market before darting out the back exit. The flow of large groups coming in slowed her down, but she quickly made her way through and out the door.

When Buck arrived she was nowhere to be seen.

Carefully, he moved out of the entranceway and headed back toward the filled parking lot. Once he moved past the closed machine shop, people became scarce, being directed to use a different designated parking area.

Glancing over his shoulder, he moved between the rows of cars, farther away from the sounds of the congested crowds, until the silence fell heavily on the parked vehicles. Bending down on one knee Buck reached up into the bottom of his left pant leg and took the small Ruger out of its holster. The silencer slid on easily. Dropping to all fours he looked underneath the cars, searching for a pair of shapely legs.

A bullet whizzed by his head, grazing the car next to him. Buck looked over his shoulder and saw a blond man with a malicious grin. He was using both outstretched arms to hold the gun pointed in Buck's direction.

"You again?" Buck said. "Who the hell are you?"

He scampered around the front of the car, wedging himself between the bumpers of two parked cars.

Slowly he lifted his head. Buck tried to see the man through the windows, but the different sizes of the vehicles made it difficult. He peeked out from the side and saw the guy coming toward him.

The window of a hard-top Jeep shattered directly in front of the stranger, taking both him and Buck by surprise. The blond stopped, looking off to his right, and when Buck changed focus, he saw Mrs. Truque taking aim at the unknown assailant.

"What is this," Buck mumbled, "an assassination round robin?" An adrenaline-fueled smile crossed his lips.

Not expecting another target, he raised his arm in Buck's direction and took a quick shot.

A woman's scream interrupted the moment. All three of the gun holders turned to the unexpected sound. A woman was watching the proceedings and had let out a blood-curdling yell. She pointed in the direction of the three of them and ran into the flea market to get help.

Another round of silent fire whizzed by Buck's head. The blond man had obviously recovered from the surprise.

Agent 98 ducked as the car behind him clanged and leaked fluid from being hit by the bullet. He leapt across the open aisle and fired his gun at the retreating figure. Another shot followed from somewhere else. Buck landed next to a car and quickly crawled underneath. Peering from below the metal undercarriage, he saw a pair of feminine legs in flat shoes walk by. He slid his gun forward and fired at the feet. They jumped and ran off out of sight.

Taking the momentary advantage, Buck crawled out from underneath the car. Leaning down, he crept around to the side and hugged close against the driver's door. Slowly he stood, looking through the rows of car windows. Not seeing anyone, he cautiously pulled himself up and looked over the metallic rooftops. He shielded his eyes from the reflective glare.

"She couldn't have disappeared."

"She didn't," the voice said from behind him. "Now drop the gun."

Buck felt the pistol's edge press into the nape of his neck. The click of the hammer being cocked sounded loudly in his ear. His Ruger fell to his feet.

"I could blow your head off right now, Agent 98," she cooed into his ear. "My, how the mighty have fallen."

Chapter Twenty

What is that stench in the air?" Buck said, sniffing loudly. "It smells of cheap vodka and bitter loneliness. That can only mean one thing."

Buck spun around so he could look her in the eye. The pistol never moved and was now pointing at his throat.

"The return of Miss Noxia von Tüssëll," he loudly proclaimed.

A genuine smile crossed his face at the sight of his best friend and rival within the Agency.

"I have so many questions for you, Barbe Truque," Buck said. "Good name, by the way."

"Thanks," Agent 46 said. She lowered the gun and released the hammer. "When did you get it figured out?"

"It struck me as an odd name from the start," Agent 98 answered. "Everyone said you were French, so I looked it up in the dictionary. Barbe Truque? 'Beard—False.' That's one even I'm envious of, and I can be pretty good with aliases."

"I know," she answered. "I still like Noxia the best. And I'm guessing you're still calling Agent 69 Muffin?"

He nodded. "This is why you always turn up back at work every October looking finely coiffed and tanned, and your hair perfectly tinted."

"And nobody here has seen me any other way than I am now."

"Why the blue lenses?" Buck asked, a stunned look still on his face.

"I thought it would go better with the blond hair."

"Huh," Buck said. "All this time I thought it was a yearly tune-up at a fat farm. Who knew?"

"Thanks. Thanks for that." Agent 46 smiled at her friend, giving him a looking over.

"That shirt looks great on you," she said. "What color is that, aubergine?"

Buck flew into her arms, hugging her tightly.

"God bless you for knowing that," he whispered. "God bless you!"

"If you're done with all the sentiment," she said. Confusion crept into her voice. Patting him on the back, she signaled the end of their embrace. "We should get out of here before the police arrive. Muffin won't be happy if we're found."

"Agreed!" Buck said. He opened his wallet and threw a hundred-dollar bill through the broken window of the Jeep. "It wasn't their fault."

"The blond guy back there," Noxia asked, catching her breath. "Was he a friend of yours?"

"I have no idea who he was," Buck answered. "But either he or his twin jumped me and left me in a gator swamp as bait."

"That poor alligator," she said with a wink. "Let's head back into the market. I doubt he'll try to shoot us within a group. I think he ran off after the woman screamed, but I can't be certain. There's at least safety in the crowd."

They darted their way through the maze of cars without being seen. As they reached the entrance, several security guards rushed past them heading for the parking area.

The agents casually walked back into the throngs of people.

"Now tell me," Buck said. He was certain the noisy surroundings would drown out any chance of them being overheard. "What the hell are you doing here?"

"Where do you want me to start?"

"Why not at the very beginning?" Buck sang. "I've always heard it's a good place to start."

"Always the show queen, Maria," Noxia replied with a heavy sigh. "I should have shot you when I had the chance."

"Don't be a bitch," Buck said.

The word slipped out before he could stop it, instantly knowing the mistake was made. The pain shot up his arm as Agent 46 squeezed his hand with a vise-like grip.

"You know I hate that word," she whispered.

"Understood," he squeaked out.

"I've known Miguel Reyes since he was just starting his political career," she explained, lessening her hold on his hand. "That was a year before I started my training at the Agency. I used to be his beard at formal events. When he asked me to fill in as a summer tutor for Alejandro, I couldn't say no."

"Still playing the bearded lady, *oui*?"

"That's why I thought it was clever," she said. "Spanish is much more prevalent than French, in northern Florida at least. I doubted anyone would do that much homework."

They made another turn down another crowded pathway.

"How come I didn't recognize you?" Buck asked. "I've known you *many*, and I do mean *many* years."

"One of the reasons the Agency loves me is because I'm a chameleon."

"Reptilian maybe," Buck said. "I wouldn't necessarily be so specific."

"While most people have some sense of how to avoid being seen," she explained, ignoring the comment, "I seem to have a talent for it. It's how I can move in and out of so many social circles without having them come crashing together."

"And here I thought you were just overly anal retentive keeping everything painfully separate."

"That too."

"Now for the big question," Buck said. "Why the hell didn't Muffin just give you the assignment and leave me out of it? You all know I hate kids."

"We know. First of all…" Noxia paused in midsentence. She continued in a rapid breath. "I'm too close to the situation." She opened her mouth to say something else but stopped herself, closing it again without another word.

Buck waited for her to continue as they walked along. After several long moments, nothing more was said.

"And second of all?" he finally prompted.

"There is no second," she answered firmly. "I'm just too close to the situation to be first-string here."

Buck gave her a sideways glance, deciding to let it drop.

"Does anyone else know about your undercover work?" he hesitantly asked. "Anyone else at the beach house?"

"No," Noxia answered. "Just Miguel. There's no reason for anyone else to know anything else. It would compromise too much. I think it's best if everyone, including Miguel, thinks I've skipped town."

"It would have saved me a lot of time if someone told me at the beginning," Buck said.

"You were told," she confirmed. "Both Agent 69 and Miguel tried to indirectly lead you away from me as a suspect."

"Next time have them be more direct."

"That's your own fault," she chided with a chuckle. "Now tell me, what do you know so far?"

Buck filled her in on the past twenty-four hours.

"That's not a lot," she said with a disparaging tone.

"Yeah," Buck said. "Well, I didn't know you were you until early this morning."

They turned another corner.

"I actually knew that about Phynilla's brother," Noxia said.

"Oh you did not," Buck snapped at her.

"Actually, I did. The Pilgrim's Church has been on my radar for quite some time. They've been extremely active vocally since

Miguel took office. I found a reference to their relationship in an interview Reverend Walker did about his father. They only have a mother in common."

"Since you brought her up," Buck said with an instigating nudge of his head, "what do you think of her?"

"Phynilla?" Noxia answered. "I like her fine. Once you get to know her you can see how determined she is to succeed at whatever she does. I wouldn't get in her way for something she wants, and I wouldn't doubt her loyalty to the governor. Although I think that's more loyalty to her job; who the governor was would be irrelevant. I knew the two of you would clash. That's why I arranged for her to pick you up."

"Thanks for that."

"Well, someone had to take you down a peg," Noxia said. "Otherwise you'd start this mission on some high-and-mighty soapbox, and nothing would get done."

"I have a question for you," Buck asked.

"I don't know why I do it," she said. "It just makes me smile."

"Not that. Where are we going?"

Agent 46 stopped walking and pointed to a restaurant at the far end of the row. The flag waving above proclaimed it Aunt Sally's Home-style Cooking.

"Muffin is meeting us inside."

Chapter Twenty-one

R oll out the barrel," Agent 69 said. The two other agents approached the table. "The gang's all here."

"Great," Noxia said to Buck. "Now you've got *him* singing, too?"

Agent 69 sat alone at a picnic table along the back wall. People bustled through the large tent with long wooden tables jaggedly spaced across the hay-strewn ground. Servers wearing bib overalls or red-and-white-checkered blouses and skirts darted through the crowd like silverfish.

"As if you didn't know that Noxia was Mrs. Truque," Buck replied. He slid onto the bench next to the portly man.

"Still using that name, I see. Agent 46," Muffin said stoically. "Must you bring to lunch the trash you pick up?"

"Sorry, Agent 69," Noxia replied. "But you know how he'll follow anything with a nice ass."

"Hello?" Buck said. "I'm sitting right here. And who ever told you that you have a nice ass?"

"All right now," Muffin said. "Agent 46, has Buck brought you up to speed?"

"As far as I know," she replied.

"Actually," Buck said. He paused as the waiter approached the table.

A handsome collegiate man with dark blond hair and wearing

blue denim overalls over a tight white T-shirt greeted the three of them. His left strap hung unfastened.

"I'm just going to make this easy," Muffin said to the other agents. He turned to the waiting young man. "Three of the fried chicken platters."

"Is that with all the fixins'?" he asked, adding in his own accentuation.

"Sure," Agent 69 stumbled. "All the fix-ins."

Buck grabbed the man's arm before he left the table. "Please tell me you serve liquor," he said hopefully.

"Beer and wine," was the perky reply.

"I'll have a draft beer," Buck said.

"House red, please," Noxia said simultaneously.

"Iced tea," Muffin said a moment behind. "Unsweetened."

"You were about to say something?" Noxia asked. "Not that that's anything unusual."

"At least I get my job done."

"Good for you," Noxia added. "I look forward to the eventual notification."

"Stop it," Muffin snapped. "Why is it whenever you two are together, I feel like I should be spanking you and sending you to bed without dinner?"

"Dibs on the spanking," Buck said. His hand shot up in the air. "Please, sir!"

"Will you just tell us what you've learned?" Muffin asked.

"What are the magic words?" Buck baited.

"Bite me?"

"And Muffin gets one out," Buck replied with a good-natured smile. "I found out that there have been threats made to Governor Miguel Reyes in the past."

"You mean those calls that came into his office a few years back?" Noxia sounded surprised. "They never panned out to anything and stopped as soon as the media got hold of it."

"Not entirely true," Buck said. "Peter Sarto was the guy who was investigated."

"What happened?" asked Agent 69.

"Several threats were made over the phone," Agent 98 explained. "When Miguel first took office. They threatened to kill him or kidnap members of his family. The first threat was made to kidnap his daughter."

"He doesn't have one," Agent 46 further explained to Muffin.

"That's why they didn't take it seriously," Buck continued.

The server came over with three big red plastic baskets each lined with a paper napkin and piled high with pieces of fried chicken, a mountain of fries, and half dozen hush puppies.

"Enjoy," he said, placing down the food and the drinks. He spun on his heels and disappeared into the crowd.

"Is this lunch or a slow version of murder?" Muffin asked, gazing over the food. "I think they forgot the extra helping of deep-fried lard."

"So you're not going to eat those hush puppies?" Buck asked, his fork poised in midair.

"Whatever happened to Peter Sarto?" Muffin asked. He rolled his eyes and slid his plate over.

"If memory serves correctly," Noxia said.

"And it does," all three simultaneously answered.

"Who came up with that?" Muffin asked.

"I did!" Buck and Noxia answered simultaneously.

They shared a collective chuckle at the shared synergy.

"He was looked into as a suspect," she continued. "But there was no concrete proof. The phone booth was checked for prints, but there were so many that nothing could be determined."

"Why was he even a suspect?" Buck asked.

"The place where he worked was under surveillance for a series of hate crimes," Noxia explained. "The owner of an electrician company called the Current Sea was a known Klansman named Marc Behr."

"They still exist?" Buck said, aghast.

"More than you know," Agent 69 said. "According to our reports, the Klan is still very active. More politically behind the scenes than burning crosses these days, but they are still an active force in the South."

"Exactly." Noxia said. "Peter was photographed using the phone booth on several occasions. He was investigated and let go because all of the evidence was circumstantial."

"You do know the governor's history, don't you?" Buck said.

"It's kind of my job," she answered. "What's that look for?"

"Nothing," Buck replied. He scrutinized her, his narrow-eyed stare boring into her.

"Stop it." She shifted on her bench. "You're making me feel uncomfortable."

"Whatever happened to the owner?" Agent 69 asked.

"During Peter's investigation all threatening calls stopped," she concluded. "They were pretty sure Peter made them, but couldn't prove it. The company shut down shortly after. It was all looked into at the time and nothing came of it."

"Agent 98," Muffin said. He wiped his lips, pushing away the basket of chicken bones. "You do the background checks and research on Peter Sarto. He may not be connected at all, but it won't hurt to see what he's been up to. Find out what happened with the electrician company and see if you can find out who the owners are now."

"I can do that," Buck said. "And what's next for Mrs. Truque here?"

Noxia smiled and dabbed at her bronzed lips with the napkin. "I'm staying out of sight," she said. "As I told you earlier, I'm working on an investigation dealing with the Pilgrim's Church."

"What are you looking into?" Buck asked.

"I can't say right now," Noxia answered. "I'm superstitious and don't want to tempt fate."

"What is Reverend Walker's deal, anyway?"

"He was in a car accident when he was twenty-one years old," Noxia answered. "He survived and the passenger didn't. He claimed that God saved him and sent him a message as a warning. He's been a zealot ever since."

"What was the message?"

"He never said," Noxia answered. "At least not that I can find so far."

"Not an untypical story," Buck said. "Survival in a life-changing incident causing religious awakening. It's almost clichéd."

"Who was the passenger?" Agent 69 asked.

"A man named Leroy White. They were the same age and best friends. Leroy was pronounced DOA at the hospital."

"And Clarence blames himself," Buck concluded. "That explains that."

Agent 46 didn't comment. She raised her eyebrows and shrugged.

"Okay," Agent 69 concluded. "I guess this wraps up this reunion."

"How do I get in touch with you, Noxia?" Buck asked.

"You don't," she said with a spiteful grin. "You contact Muffin and he'll contact me."

"Don't you trust me?" Buck asked.

"No," she answered easily. "But that has nothing to do with it. It's a precaution in case something happens to your phone. No tracebacks."

"Got it."

"Go forth, my children," Agent 69 said. He raised his hands and held them palms turned out as if offering a blessing. "Be fruitful—no commentary, Buck—and may you both be successful."

"I hate it when he feels sanctimonious," Buck said to Noxia, getting up from the table. "Don't you?"

CHAPTER TWENTY-TWO

Hey," said the plump African American woman as she opened the door. "You must be Mrs. Truque."

"Yes, I am," she answered, putting out her hand. "Thank you for having me over, Miss Etheridge."

"You can call me Norma," the curvaceous woman said. She gave her a once-over look from head to foot and back before stepping aside and holding open the door.

"Barbe, thank you," Mrs. Truque responded in kind. She handed her a card with her name and phone number on it. "Is that Etheridge, like Melissa?"

"Yeah." Norma led the way into a pleasantly decorated room. "She's my second cousin." She paused before laughing at her own joke. Taking a seat at one end of the blue-cloth-covered sofa, she motioned for Barbe to sit. A wicker table with a centerpiece throw rug underneath was set with a sweating pitcher of ice water and two glasses. The rug's colorful design complemented the pale bamboo of the table and the dark wooden floors.

"I have to admit I was thrown by your call," she said.

"I appreciate the fact that you're willing to talk to me at all," Mrs. Truque said. "It took me a while to find any of Leroy's friends. Most have moved away. I tried to call his mother, but she said she wouldn't discuss it. I guess she doesn't want to relive it. I can't very well blame her. It must be difficult to lose a child.

Anyway, she eventually gave me your name and I found your email address."

Norma sat on the edge of the couch. Her plump thighs stretched the limits of her XL denim shorts. A black T-shirt hugged tightly to her ample bosom and an open navy blue button-down shirt covered her shoulders with the sleeves rolled up to her elbows.

"His mom took it hard," Norma said. She ran a hand through the magenta-dyed bangs on an otherwise shorn head. "She got all religious and shit."

"I'm sorry," Mrs. Truque said. "May I have some water?"

"Please," Norma answered. She poured two glasses, handing one to Barbe.

"What do you mean she got religious?"

"She wasn't really that religious before the car accident," Norma said. "In fact, she was pretty cool. Very supportive of Leroy and his friends."

"Where were you on the night of January sixth?" she asked. Quickly she softened. "If you don't mind?"

"I don't mind," said Norma. The big golden hoops danced from her ears; they matched the golden cross that was nestled above her deep cleavage. "You sure you ain't a cop? 'Cause you sound like one."

"No," Barbe said with a smile. She took a sip of the ice water. "I'm not a police officer. I'm a reporter doing an article on drunk driving. This case caught my attention and I thought I'd use it as an example."

"I have one question before we start," Norma said. Her bold-red-painted lips rested at a pout.

"What's that?"

"I want to know why you would drive two hours, crossing state lines, to discuss a drunk driving accident that happened over fifteen years ago."

Mrs. Truque raised her eyebrows and shrugged. "I've already

told you. I'm doing a report." She added, "I'm happy to pay you for your time."

"Fine by me." Norma dismissed her curiosity. "Leroy was a good friend and he'd like to be remembered."

"Where were you that night?"

"I was bouncing the door at the Jade Star," Norma recalled. "Leroy was there with three of the regular guys. They'd hang out by the door and keep me company sometimes."

"Were they drunk?" Mrs. Truque asked, sitting calmly on the couch.

Her long legs were crossed at the ankles and ended in a pair of comfortable shoes. She wore a pair of blue jeans that accentuated her shape without hugging to her form. The peach-colored pullover brought out the blue eyes and the strawberry highlights in the blond hair that hung to her shoulders.

"The accident wasn't CJ's fault," Norma defensively said. "He was driving. They were lookin' sober when they left the bar. It was some other asshole that slammed into them."

"I'm not here to accuse anyone," Mrs. Truque said. "It says they weren't at fault in the report."

"There was a lot of stuff said back then," Norma said. "They tried to make it out like it was CJ's fault because the other car was driven by some white boy. He weren't even scratched up that bad. A few broken bones and maybe some scrapes. That was all. CJ's leg was broke and Leroy died."

"Who is CJ again?" Mrs. Truque asked. She held her glass tightly, hoping her anticipation didn't show. Holding her breath, she waited for an answer.

"That's CJ Walker," Norma replied. She leaned forward to refill her glass. She cut a quick glance at Mrs. Truque, admiring her figure, before she sat back down. "CJ and Leroy were *very close.*"

"Do you, by chance," Mrs. Truque leaned forward, coiling her neck like a swan, knowing how to work one of her best feminine assets, "have any pictures of Leroy? Maybe of Leroy and CJ?"

"Girl, please!" Norma leaned forward until their faces were six inches apart. Barbe noticed her nose twitch as she smelled the rich dark amber of Barbe's perfume. "If there's a picture of Leroy, you can bet CJ was in it!"

Norma reached behind her back and pulled her cell phone from her back pocket. Using it as an excuse she slid next to Mrs. Truque, pressing thigh against thigh. Her phone's screen flashed on, revealing an erect, muscled red fist with a small red bar crossing just above the elbow, turning it into a powerful symbol of Venus.

"After my girlfriend and I broke up," Norma explained, "I was cleaning out the closet and found a box of these photos. It took me a while but I got a bunch of them loaded up to my Facebook page."

She took a moment to flip through her phone.

"Here ya go." Norma's pudgy fingers held out the phone.

Four young men were captured laughing and having an evening completely free of care as only boys in their early twenties can do. Two waifish youths stood on either side of another couple, all with their arms linked around each other's shoulders. The boys in the center intimately rested their heads against one another.

"The Jade Star," Mrs. Truque asked with surprise. "It was a gay bar?"

She pulled the phone closer to study the photo. It was then she noticed the fine line between waifish youth and youthful homosexual male.

"I don't mean to sound so surprised," Barbe explained. "Since there aren't any bars there now, I didn't think there ever were any in Tallahassee."

Norma slowly pulled herself up to sitting fully erect. She rested her elbows on her knees.

"Yeah," she slowly answered. "This wasn't in Tallahassee.

It was here in Georgia. The Jade Star went out of business about a year after this picture was taken."

"And that's Leroy and CJ Walker." Mrs. Truque pointed to each boy as she said his name. "There in the center."

"Yeah," Norma answered. Her defenses slowly lowered again.

"Are you absolutely sure of that?"

"Hell yeah," Norma said. "I'm the one that took that picture. 'Shine on!' they used to say. 'Shine on!' I remember it like it was yesterday."

Mrs. Truque's head snapped around to stare directly at Norma. She quickly reached for her water glass and took a sip, trying to hide her surprise.

"How long were CJ and Leroy a couple?" she asked, letting a purr creep into her voice.

Norma stopped to think for a moment.

"By that time." She retrieved her phone from Barbe's hands, making sure their hands touched. "I knew them about a year. They were together before I met them."

"Would you do me a favor and email me a copy of that picture?" Mrs. Truque asked with a coy smile. "You have my address. Feel free to use as high a resolution as you possibly can. I can handle it." She slowly blinked, flirting.

Norma's boldly red-painted lips curved into a smile. "No problem, doll."

Norma let the title hang in the air between them. When she didn't get any discouragement, her smile increased and her fingers got busy sending the photo.

"Thanks, Norma," Mrs. Truque said.

She proudly sat back on the couch, her smile interrupted only by taking a drink of water. Suddenly her eyes grew round and the corners of her mouth curled wider with impish delight. "Any idea what happened to CJ after the accident?"

"Nay," Norma replied. She hit send on the phone. "I heard he found religion. Moved away to Florida somewhere."

"Any clue as to where?"

"I'm a Georgia girl," Norma said. Her eyes locked on Barbe's subtle pout. "I don't have any business going into Florida. I got enough trouble here."

Mrs. Truque sat forward, pressing against Norma's leg. She let her arm lightly traipse its way up her back, resting on the navy blue collar by Norma's neck.

"Norma," she salaciously solicited, "do you have plans for tomorrow afternoon?"

"That depends on what you had in mind, doll."

"Meet me tomorrow in Tallahassee."

"Girl," Norma said. "Didn't you hear what I just told you? I. Don't. Go. Into. Florida. Sorry, but that's just the way it is. What did you want me to do anyway?"

"Sit onstage holding the photograph of Leroy," Mrs. Truque explained. "During the governor's rally tomorrow."

"Ain't that the gay governor?"

"Yes!"

Norma thought a moment and then shook her head.

"Nay," she said firmly. "I don't like the sound of that. I saw that movie *Milk*, the one about that mayor getting shot. With my luck, the bullet will miss the target and shoot me. Don't you see the movies? The black girl will always get it first, I don't care if he is Hispanic. There ain't no way I'm going to Florida."

Mrs. Truque studied Norma as she stubbornly sat with her arms firmly crossed beneath her large breasts.

"Okay," she decided. She stood up and dug her hand into her pocket. She took out a small fold of bills. Counting out two hundred dollars, she held it out for Norma.

"Thank you very much," she said. "You don't know how helpful you've been."

"I don't see how," Norma replied. "Anyways, you're the one who helped me." She shoved the money into her pocket and patted the denim after for reassurance.

Mrs. Truque said good-bye again at the door before walking to her car. She never looked over her shoulder but had the distinctive feeling of being watched. Barbe Truque smiled when opening the door of her green Miata and politely waved.

Taking out her cell phone, she dialed the familiar digits. It rang twice before Buck answered with a snide comment.

"Not much, Kitten," was Mrs. Truque's snarky reply. "Did you have a good day at school?"

CHAPTER TWENTY-THREE

B uck sat at a back table in the sparsely populated video bar. With his iPad propped before him, he looked up as the handsome waiter brought his drink. The evening was late and this particular bar extremely quiet for a Saturday.

"Thank you," Buck said with a flirtatious smile. He looked from the waiter to his lemon drop, visually letting both wet his lips.

"May I get you anything else?" the dark-haired young man offered.

"Yes," Buck said with a salacious smile. "Yes, you may, but for now I'll settle for an open tab." He handed the man his credit card with a wink.

Buck took a sip of his cocktail as the waiter returned behind the dark wooden bar. The iPad connected to the Internet by means of a private filter for security reasons, avoiding all ways to trace his work. He tapped the letters P-e-t-e-r -S-a-r-t-o into the Google search engine, then flipped through the pages of advertisements to get to the linked articles. After two pages he found one of interest and clicked on the link. The page exploded into focus. The *Tallahassee Democrat* newspaper's headline boldly declared:

HATE CRIME CALLS MADE AGAINST GOVERNOR

Agent 98 scanned the article, looking for any factors he hadn't heard at lunch; he didn't find any. With another sip of his drink Buck looked over the black-and-white photograph on the front page of the daily broadsheet.

Even digitally enhanced the picture still appeared grainy. A series of snapshots showing a man walking toward, getting into, and using the phone booth preceded another set of the same man leaving. The face was circled in two photos with a line leading away to a circled close-up in the upper right-hand corner. Printed underneath was the name Peter Sarto.

"Nothing much to look at," Buck mumbled.

Another sip of his cocktail inspired a new idea. Going to the search bar, he typed in the name that Noxia had mentioned earlier: Marc Behr.

The page went blank before bursting into colorful blue links followed by tiny black lettering.

Scanning over the headlines he searched through several articles only to find a limited retelling of the same story, connecting the owner of the Current Sea electrical to Klan activity around the state of Florida and up into southern Georgia. Many black-and-white photos of Mr. Behr in civilian clothes alongside one of him in Klan formal wear dotted the listings as thumbnails waiting to be opened.

Marc Behr looked average in height in comparison to others in the photographs. His body was round and stout, matching his fleshy face and full cheeks. Piggish eyes twinkled out from a closely shaved head, and his beard was trimmed to a triangular point. In some pictures the beard was braided, resembling a twig jutting off his chin at an odd angle.

Buck was about to click on the next page when an article title caught his attention at the very bottom of the listings. Curious, he tapped the link, letting it open the report titled "Klansman Receives City Award."

Written after the Current Sea closed, the article described how Marc Behr was given a city award as Businessman of the

Year, four years before the alleged threats were made from the phone booth outside his company's office. It went on to expose not only the public knowledge of Behr's Klan activity, but also the cover-up and burial of information of his alleged personal connections to certain crimes in the area. The article described how within six months after the "Phone Booth Scandal," the Current Sea closed when employees were overheard on a jobsite making bigoted remarks about the property owners.

Buck scrolled down and a color photo appeared. Mr. Behr stood on the left shaking hands and accepting a plaque from the Florida's previous, Republican administrator, Governor Cox. Both men looked directly out toward the camera with plastic grins fixed to their faces, the plaque equally held between them. Underneath was the printed caption: *Scandal would ruin both within two years.*

"Wait a minute," Buck said.

His fingers pushed the picture to center view. With another swipe he enlarged the color photo. The two men were centrally positioned in front of a backdrop with almost the entire company logo in view. It was the first time he had seen the company design in a color photograph.

Three blue waves of electricity zigzagged across the background, one on top of another, creating a nautical effect. At an angle placed above the top current was a yellow wall socket with a pole jutting out, and a single sail hung from it. The company's name was proudly written in cursive letters, floating in the electrical current.

"Isn't that familiar?" Buck muttered.

Taking another inspirational sip of his lemon drop, he saved the color photo as a screen shot, placing it in the upper corner of the iPad's desktop. He finished off the cocktail and signaled the handsome bartender for another to be delivered to the table. It was brought over as the next page pulled up.

"That last one was lip-smacking good," Buck said, demonstrating the fact.

"Those lips shouldn't be smacked," replied the young man. "They should be handcuffed and spanked."

"Suddenly," Buck said, watching the bartender return to his station, "I don't feel so old anymore." He turned his attention back to the mini computer screen. "Let's check you out, shall we?"

Agent 98 entered his security password for exclusive access to the private business reports. First, he typed in the state, then the city, and finally the company name.

UnCharted Construction was formed three years ago by its current owner, Mr. Billy Carriway. Since that time four complaints had been submitted to Florida's Better Business Bureau; no commentaries were ever entered on UnCharted's behalf, leaving all accusations unsettled. One instance was cited by the city itself. Mr. Carriway built his private residence on a hill and promptly removed the deeply rooted trees so he could enjoy the view. Unfortunately, since the trees were no longer there, the ground washed away during the autumn rains, creating a landslide onto the houses below. Mr. Carriway quickly settled the issue out of court.

"That's not a good record," Buck said. "Why didn't Miguel check them out? Oh, I see. Governor Cox kept it out of the public reports."

He continued to read through the listings, finding a small picture of the UnCharted logo listed at the bottom. The picture enlarged and was immediately moved next to the previously saved Current Sea logo for comparison.

Only a few differences were evident between the two pictures. If the floating electric socket was changed to a boat, and the words of the company rearranged, the logos would be practically identical.

"That's not enough for evidence," Agent 98 whispered, staring at the screen. "But it is enough to check it out."

Buck opened another screen and brought up UnCharted's website. Several photos existed of various employees, but none of the owner. He scrolled through the pages of customer praises until the last page was drawn. At the bottom was a group photo, showing about twenty people in four rows. The caption below read: *The Entire Crew at UnCharted Construction.*

Tapping the picture until it filled the screen, Buck snatched the iPad in both hands, studying it as closely as possible. He scanned over the listing but didn't see Billy Carriway's name there.

"That's odd." Agent 98 took note. "I've never seen a company website where the president wasn't pictured somewhere."

Buck leaned back against the banquette cushion, taking his cocktail in hand and trying to think of his next move. His eyes absently scanned over the picture, looking at the names and faces.

Agent 98 sat bolt upright to the table without spilling his drink. Practically putting his nose against the screen, he counted the faces in the back row and counted the names listing each one in place. There were twenty names listed. There were four rows of people with five people in each except for the back row, where there were six faces staring back. Enlarging the picture as much as possible without losing focus, Buck studied each face, lining them up with the names listed.

"It's as if he ran to the back row," Buck deduced. "Ducking into the photo before the camera's timer went off."

The second face from the right end was out of place. It appeared slightly blurred while the rest were completely in focus.

"I owe you one, Noxia." Buck smiled. "If it weren't for you I'd never give chameleons a second thought."

The face in the photograph was thinner and the hair grown out to show the dishwater blond. The beard was gone but a shadow was cast on the chin, allowing the resemblance to be noticed. The telltale sign was the man's eyes; those piggish eyes were unmistakable.

Without a doubt Billy Carriway and Marc Behr were the same man.

As if on cue, his Audra McDonald ringtone sounded. He looked at the caller ID, recognized the number, and answered Agent 69's call with a wicked smile.

"What's up, Daddy?" he purred into the phone.

"Not much, Kitten," was Noxia's instant reply. "Did you have a good day at school?"

"You really know how to ruin a mood," Buck said. "Why are you calling from Muffin's phone?"

"I'm not," she answered. "My phone calls are all routed through his so they can't be traced to me. Safety precaution. You really should pay more attention to the memos."

"Well, you are right on the mark," Buck teased. "Literally. You aren't going to believe what I've found out about that guy you mentioned, Marc Behr."

He proceeded to gush forth the information he'd discovered.

"That's interesting," Noxia replied slowly. Her tone was full of thought.

"Now," Buck continued, "I'm going to need you to do me a favor."

"Make it good," Agent 46 replied. "'Cause I have a whopper to tell you."

"Tomorrow afternoon I need you to go to the office of UnCharted Construction and poke around. See if you can find anything out of the ordinary."

"It's Sunday," she said after a moment.

"Yes, that's good," Buck said in a condescending tone. "It is Sunday. It's usually what follows Saturday."

"Not the best way to get me to do a favor. Why do I have to do it?"

Buck's answer was immediate. "You are so much better at picking locks and being much more inconspicuous than I."

"Hurricane Sandy was more inconspicuous than you," Noxia said. "And right now, blew less wind up my skirt. Why can't you do it?"

"I'll be with the governor at the rally in the morning," Buck answered. "I have something else I need to work on tomorrow afternoon."

A long beat of silence passed between them.

"You have a date, don't you?" It was an accusation more than a question.

"Kind of sort of," Buck started.

"Weren't you the one," Agent 46 cut him off, "who always said, and I do believe this is a quote, 'Saving the world gets in the way of all relationships'?"

"You don't know what it's like," Buck said defensively. "You're not a man."

"Give me a pair of handcuffs, a stick for you to bite on, and a dull knife, and you won't be much of one either!"

"You talk so sweetly, Mrs. Bobbitt," Buck said. "You and Phynilla should compare notes. The rally doesn't begin until noon. I'll be there for the beginning and will cut out as soon as the governor starts to speak."

"Don't you think you should be there for the entire thing?" Noxia's sarcasm dripped through the phone wire.

"Why?" Buck asked. "I'm not his personal security. I'm here for a different mission altogether."

"And what was that mission again?" Noxia asked. "Look, Buck, don't fuck around. I love that boy like…well, like he was my own."

"I bet," Buck said. His mind was racing.

"Buck, this is important…"

"So'ry," Buck said choppily into the phone. "Yu…br'king up. Ca…ear yu."

"Cut the shit, Agent 98," Noxia yelled into the phone. "I'll do what you asked. But you're going to owe me one."

"All right, I'll owe you one."

"And this is how you're going to pay me back." Noxia explained what she wanted done.

"And that's all?" Buck said, waiting for the other shoe to drop. "Sounds a little noiresque, if you ask me."

"That's why no one asked you," Noxia said. "You'll be at the rally anyway. Just go over and deliver the message. You can do me the favor and still have time for your hookup."

"Excuse me. It's a date."

"Really?" Noxia waited for an answer. "Yeah, just what I thought. All you have to do is deliver the message and walk away."

"How do you expect me to do that?" Buck asked, the sarcasm noted in his voice.

"It's an easy task. The right foot goes ahead and then the left one follows..."

"It's not going to be that easy getting that close," Buck argued.

"Try something different." Noxia paused. "Be subtle."

"Why can't you do this?" Buck asked.

"Because, fool," Noxia said. Despite being seen by no one else, her lips curled into a Cheshire Cat grin. "I'll be checking out UnCharted Construction's home office."

"Done." Buck capitulated.

"Good," Noxia said. She sounded exasperated. "Now I have a two-hour drive ahead of me. We can compare notes tomorrow."

"A two-hour drive?"

"Yu...br'king up. Ca...ear yu." She disconnected the call.

"You do like your cryptic messages, don't you?"

Agent 98 put down the phone and picked up the cocktail glass. Tilting his head back, he emptied its contents with one shot. Looking at the bartender, Buck licked his lips, uncertain which whetted his desire more.

Chapter Twenty-four

"Hallelujah!" Reverend Clarence Walker declared.

He put his pen down, beaming at his work as he imagined God had done, looking over Eden on the sixth day of Creation. As he read over his sermon his full lips moved, silently praising each written word as Gospel. Taking the pen back in his hand, he swept over the top of the page, titling the speech in large and flowing cursive.

The Sacrifice of Isaac; Today's Protection of Children!

Reverend Walker took a sip of his red wine, giving into the reward of a job well done. He always liked to write his sermons out in longhand. It felt more like the Holy Spirit guiding his hand, inspiring his work with direct communication. Much better than the informal clacking of fingers on a keyboard. Feeling the Spirit ebbing away, he closed the notebook before turning his attention to the computer on his desk.

For a brief moment the reverend's reflection showed in the dark glass. The tight black curls of hair gave way to a high forehead. The smooth molasses-colored skin revealed his dark brown eyes reflecting out from behind rectangular glass lenses. His nose gently sloped, giving way to large round nostrils that flared whenever his sermons changed from words to inspiration.

A single stroke of the keys lit up the monitor, showing a beautiful rendition of an African Jesus. Reverend Walker ran a hand over his mouth, feeling the triangular mustache covering his full lips and connecting to the goatee beard that outlined his chin. He stared at the screen Savior's image, admiring the fiery strength in the brown eyes and inspirational beauty of The Man himself. Hesitantly, he made the mouse click on a file in the corner and the picture disappeared.

An outline of Tallahassee's City Hall replaced the image on the screen. Clarence used his mouse to zoom in until he had the front of the Capitol Building and the open field leading up to the steps filling the monitor.

"If he's speaking here..." Reverend Walker whispered to the computer screen. He used the mouse's arrow to pinpoint the spot on the map. "Then the best position to be in would be...spread out in this area."

The arrow glided over the large open field in front of the building. Random clicks of the mouse left an "X" behind as a marker. Soon the boldface letter appeared randomly scattered through the field. He studied the diagram as if it were plans of war.

"The media is usually placed here." Clarence clicked the mouse, leaving another marker at the open field's lower left corner. "And they usually form about twenty minutes before the governor appears."

His mind clicked and whirled, churning thoughts like a distraction at the circus. He reached for the phone on the desk's edge, picking up the receiver and dialing. As the digits registered with audible chirps Clarence smiled, fully appreciating the old-school landline still used by the church. After the second ring, the phone was answered.

"Good evening," said the Reverend Clarence Walker into the receiver. "I'm going over the plans and wanted to know how many we can actually count on." He paused, listening, disappointed. "Not as many as I hoped, but we shall show our strength through the Lord's guidance. As it is written in the Scriptures, 'Now may the Lord's strength be displayed. The guilty shall *not* go unpunished, even if He must punish the children for the sin of the fathers to the third generation.' Hand to Jesus and Amen!"

He thumped his hand on the desktop, making the wineglass tremble.

"We will need to get there early," Reverend Walker instructed. "Spread throughout the crowd. Blend in discreetly. I will instruct the congregation that they are not to engage with me and are to remain dispersed throughout the field. Then once I give the signal everything will go into action. I will be up front with very little obstruction to the governor."

Clarence's mind drifted off to the mental images of his expectations. Among the cheers of the crowd, the noise of the masses around him, he heard the delicate whisper of the Angel's voice. His message was clear. Reverend Clarence Walker would be the Deliverer, proving that words were indeed sharper than any sword—except for that of the Lord. With the Bible in one hand, he was ready to accept the Lord's help with the other.

"I'll be dressed in my clergy attire, and that will distract the media," Clarence continued. "Tell them to wait for my signal. Then we show the world the power of the Lord's words."

He listened intently, his brow furrowing, as a low growl started within him.

"No!" he barked into the phone. "We go to the Capitol separately from here, *after* the regular service. Yes, that is the plan. All right, and God be with you."

He hung up the receiver and knitted his fingers together, resting them on the desk. Sitting back in his chair Reverend Walker stared at the computer screen. His mind replayed the flash protest that he envisioned, knowing all of his hard planning would not go to waste. The signs would randomly appear while the governor spoke. The Lord had led him to the Holy Land, and now Reverend Walker would keep it clean and pure.

He opened the Bible and randomly put his finger onto a

page. Reverend Clarence Walker read the passage and took it as personal reassurance from the Angels.

And God put Abraham to the test.

"Now," Reverend Walker said, "it is time for my own testing to begin."

CHAPTER TWENTY-FIVE

The gathering out front of the Capitol Building was packed full of observers, protesters, activists, and those who just wanted to be part of the action. People held up signs showing support as well as concerns for the governor and for the plans he was proposing to make for the state. Governor Reyes stood inside the doors, waiting to walk onto the steps and begin his speech to the masses that awaited him.

"I can't believe I still get nervous," Miguel said to Agent 98.

"That's a sign that you have humility," Buck reassured him. "Only a fool never doubts."

He looked at the governor, at the dark worry circles under his eyes that were hidden well enough for the cameras, but not for someone up close. Buck still saw the toll all this was taking on him despite the stress lines appearing all smoothed over.

"I want you to know," Governor Reyes leaned forward and spoke low, "I was completely prepared to veto R-65 today. I thought about it all day yesterday. I thought about it until I went to bed and during the hours I didn't sleep last night."

"Governor..." Buck started to say.

Miguel Reyes put up a hand to silence him.

"I'm not going to, Buck," he said. "And that's mainly because of two things. The first is that I don't think Alejandro would want me to give into that kind of blackmail. The other is because you asked me to trust you. And I do."

"I don't know what to say," Buck admitted humbly.

"Don't say anything," Miguel said. "Don't prove me wrong, either."

"My ego would never allow it," he answered with a cocky smile.

"That, I don't doubt at all." Miguel returned a strained smile.

"An excellent source tells me that today's rally should make a difference," Buck said. He reached out and patted Miguel's shoulder.

"That's good for your source," the governor said. "Let's hope that it makes a positive difference."

"Don't you two look like a pair of conspiring thieves?" Phynilla said as she walked up. "Governor, you're going to have to come get ready now."

"Phynilla," Miguel said. "I can't tell you how much I truly appreciate your work. You are perfection."

"My ego wouldn't allow anything else."

Buck's face lit up as his lips opened to a full-mouth grin. He gave Phynilla's arm a gentle shove.

"Shut up! I said almost the exact same thing less than two minutes ago."

"Oh Lord," Phynilla said, rolling her eyes. "If I'm thinking like him? Take me now, Lord! Take me now!"

"Okay," Miguel said. "Wish me luck."

"You'll be fine," Buck said.

"Thank you," Miguel replied. "True or not, I needed to hear that."

The two men shook hands before Governor Miguel Reyes followed his assistant to the back offices to get ready for the rally.

Buck watched them go. He looked at his watch and was glad to see it was only 11:10 a.m. The rally wouldn't start for another fifty minutes. The crowd forming out front was already an impressive size.

"Let's go get this done," he muttered. "And then on to better things."

Once outside, Buck made his way around the building and toward the lawn where the rally was going to be held. Throngs of people were already in place, packed close, standing and waiting for the governor to speak. He meandered along the outskirts of the crowd, trying to size up the number of people.

As he approached the front he saw the area roped off for the media. They, of course, were given an unobstructed view of the stage. Security carefully checked the credentials of anyone trying to enter the roped-off area. Skirting around, Buck crossed in front while scanning over the faces in the crowd.

"Bingo!" he said, finding the face he was searching for. "Now how to get there?"

Buck backtracked his route and moved up several rows along the side.

"Sorry." He repeated it often, zigzagging through the crowd and feeling like a cartoon. "Excuse me. Pardon me."

When he saw the formal black suit, Buck called out.

"Reverend Walker? Reverend Walker."

At the sound of his name, Reverend Clarence J. Walker turned, scanning the crowds around him. His vision brushed past Buck before he heard his name called again. His head snapped back and he focused on Buck with a cautious curiosity.

"Reverend Walker," Buck called out. His smile broadened when he saw the clergyman meeting his gaze.

"Yes?" he hesitantly answered.

Dressed in a fastidious black suit with a coal-colored tie against a blue shirt, he reached up to push his glasses back to the bridge of his nose.

"Do I know you?"

"No," Buck answered. "We've not met."

He pushed his way closer when the two muscular African American men on either side of the reverend stepped in front of him. Both men wore black suits and had their arms across their chests.

"That is close enough, sir," one of the men stated.

Buck halted in his path. He looked at the two men and smiled, disbelieving the need for a reverend to have bodyguards.

"Reverend Walker," Buck tried to say. He darted his head to either side, trying to see around the human gorilla in his path. "I have a message for you."

"A message for me?"

The Seminole fight song broke out and the crowd erupted in cheers. The governor walked onto the front steps to loud applause and whistling. Waving with great enthusiasm, Governor Reyes approached the podium.

"What do you mean, a message?" asked Reverend Walker. He nodded to the men to let them know it was okay. "A message from whom?"

Buck chuckled before answering. "Actually it's from Miss Noxia von Tüssëll, but I don't think you know her either."

"Obnoxious what?" The reverend was clearly not following. "I don't know who you are, and I don't know anyone by that ridiculous-sounding name."

"It's not ridiculous," Buck said. "It's German. And who gave me the message isn't the point right now."

"Then what is the point?" he asked. "I'm trying to watch the governor, if you don't mind."

"No offense," Buck said with a cocky grin. "But I think you're going to want to hear this."

"Ladies and gentlemen," the governor was saying. "Thank you for coming out on a beautiful day like today. Go 'Noles!"

The crowd erupted with linked enthusiasm.

Reverend Walker's pug expression transformed to stone.

"I've seen you." His eyes grew smaller, studying Buck as

he put the face to the place. "You're that boy that came into my church the other night. The night of our debate."

"Very good," Buck said, impressed. "I didn't think you saw me."

"You were a tad conspicuous, to say the least." He nodded to the two men flanking him. They each took a step back.

"Thank you," Buck said to both with a short grin.

He took a step forward and one of the guards intercepted him. With rapid efficiency he patted Buck down, making sure there was no threat to the clergyman.

"No dinner? No movie?" Buck shook his head. "No second date for you!"

Reverend Walker's face grew pinched. "If you don't mind," he said with distinctive sharpness, "what is the message?"

Buck leaned forward, keeping both of his hands raised by his shoulders. He paused, his lips a short distance from the reverend's ear. Buck took a deep, slow breath, making sure his breathing brushed between them. Waiting for an instant of quiet from the cheering crowds, Buck leaned in. Speaking out of the corner of his mouth, he melodramatically gave the message as if whispering a secret passcode.

"The Jade Star Shines On."

Reverend Clarence Walker jumped back, pushing Buck away. A look of pure hatred crossed his face, pinching his mouth to a pucker and locking his jaw. His eyes blazed while his nostrils flared. His chest rose and fell several times with angry control.

"What kind of demon from hell are you?" he seethed in whispered words.

"I beg your pardon?" Buck said. Shock and surprise flooded over him. He quickly pulled himself together to cover his reaction.

"What kind of game are you playing with me, boy?" Clarence snapped.

The two goons took a step closer. Buck took a step back.

"Hey," Agent 98 said. He put both hands out in front of him. "I was told to give you the message."

"You've given your message," Reverend Walker said. "Now get the hell away from me."

"Excuse me!" Buck said, very irritated. "I don't take orders from anyone unless they pull my hair first!"

"You are a vile man," Reverend Walker yelled. His eyes grew large behind the rectangular lenses, and his body shook with rage. "Degenerate in the eyes of the Lord!"

He raised his fist in anger, shaking it at Buck.

At this cue, two signs were thrust above the heads of the masses. Murmurs traveled across the lawn in waves.

THE EYES OF THE LORD
ARE IN EVERY PLACE
KEEPING WATCH ON EVIL

Another sign went up on the other side of the lawn.

REPENT AND TURN TO HIM
SO YOUR SINS MAY BE WASHED CLEAN

"No!" Reverend Walker said in a harsh whisper. He looked around as several more signs rose into the air. "Not now!"

His words were in vain as a half dozen signs with similar passages written on them were being waved above the heads.

"As it says in the Bible," Reverend Walker hissed at Buck, "woe to that man by whom He is betrayed! Vengeance is mine, sayeth the Lord!"

"Yeah, yeah," Buck said, turning to read the signs. "As it says in *Sweeney Todd*—seeking revenge leads to hell, but everyone does it."

The governor's speech slowed down as the distraction caught his eye, but he recovered quickly and continued. The pause was enough to cause the crowds, as well as the media, to look around and observe the interference. Cameras rolled on their stands to scan over the sea of people, momentarily focusing on the messages appearing throughout the crowd. The security was already wrestling a few signs from protesters.

"Now that's something, eh?" Buck turned to look for the reverend.

Reverend Clarence Walker was desperately trying to push his way through the crowd and leave the grounds of the state capitol.

CHAPTER TWENTY-SIX

I can understand that you're wanting to avoid hassles at work," Buck conceded. "But if you don't take a stand for yourself, how can you ask the governor to take one for the state?"

Buck sat in the passenger seat of the truck with his hand resting on Benjamin's knee. He was dressed in a pair of black slacks and a solid coral button-down with the sleeves rolled up to his elbows.

"I think we can find better things to do than discuss the politics of coming out at work," Benjamin said. He looked over from the driver's seat, flashing a large grin. The smile seemed brighter as it spread out under the darkened sunglasses. He wore a black open-neck pullover and a pair of khakis. Tufts of hair peeked out of the V-neck's opening.

"I wonder what will present itself." Buck let his hand drift up Benjamin's inner thigh.

"Don't tickle my leg." Benjamin gave a friendly warning. "Remember, safety first."

"You sound like a condom ad," Buck replied. His hand retreated back to the knee. "Where are we going, anyway?"

"I told you," was the reply.

"You said 'tickets.' There's a lot that falls under that banner. For all I know you could be taking me to a state patrolman's ball. Or a monster truck rally. I mean, this is the South."

"Patrolmen don't have balls."

"You said it, not me," Buck commented. "Where *are* we going? State fair? Cancún? A Night of Lesbian Poetry? Or worse yet, a Britney Spears concert?"

"I don't *think* so," Benjamin answered.

Buck looked over, his grin disappearing.

"Are you all right?" Benjamin asked. Concern swept over his voice. "You look like someone's walked on your grave."

"Nothing. It's a personal quirk, I'll explain another time," Buck answered, shrugging off the moment. He pushed past, eager to change the subject. "You were right about Jimmy."

"Oh? How's that?"

"After I left you yesterday morning," Buck said, "he was at the gate and let me in. I couldn't swear it, but I thought he made a little snide comment when I drove by."

"Oh, he did," Benjamin said decisively.

"He said something to you?"

"No," Benjamin answered. "He makes them all the time about everyone. You should hear what he says about Phynilla."

"I can only imagine," Buck said. He paused, giving Benjamin a sideways glance. "What does he say about you?"

"I don't know." Benjamin gasped with a shocked grin. "I'm not there when he says it."

"Why do you put up with that?"

"What am I supposed do?" he asked with a laugh. "We're both only employees doing our job. There's not much I *can* do, so what should I do? I hear his comments and think, 'Man. This guy's a douche nozzle.' I'd call him an asshole, but why give him false hope for advancement?"

"Point made." Buck sighed heavily. "I guess if being a security guard is as far as you're going in life, then let him have it."

"Watch it," Benjamin said. "I'm a security guard."

"You have other things to look forward to," Buck argued.

"You're studying French and want to travel. I think the most Jimmy gets to look forward to is hoping someone crashes during a NASCAR race."

"You are such a snob," Benjamin said with a laugh. "You don't know him. Jimmy may be ignorant but he has skills."

"Knowing the difference between shit and Shinola by the second guess isn't a skill."

"Very funny. He's done several things," Benjamin argued. "He was a mechanic, a construction worker..."

"I'll start singing 'YMCA' if you say policeman and Indian chief!"

"He's been a roofer," Benjamin continued. "And an electrician, and even an iron welder."

"Why are you defending a man you just called a douche nozzle?" Buck asked. "How in the world do you know all of that about him anyway?"

"Guys chat," Benjamin said. "Security can be a lot of downtime with not a lot to do. We kill the time shooting the shit. I'm just saying you shouldn't judge someone by their appearance."

"During all of these little intimate chats you've had at work," Buck said, ignoring the comment, "none of them have been able to figure out you're a big queer?"

"I do more listening than chatting when it comes to them," Benjamin confessed. "If you nod a lot and smile, grunt a few times, they pretty much will continue talking. They'll make conclusions on their own. I don't need to connect the dots for them."

"Whatever," Buck muttered, looking out the passenger window. "It's your job, not mine."

"Let's not go there again," Benjamin said. The truck turned in to a parking lot.

"Why aren't you at the rally today serving and protecting?" Buck asked, changing the subject. "Not that I'm complaining."

"Different kind of security," Benjamin answered. "Different security company. I was lucky to get the day off at all."

"Why?" Buck asked. "I'm assuming even you get a day off."

"Jimmy wanted the day off as well," Benjamin said. "He has some family thing. The backup team had to come into work on a Sunday. They weren't happy but they'll get paid well." He turned off the truck's engine. "I hope you like what I have planned."

"I'll let you know once you tell me what it is," Buck said.

"If you stop bitching for a minute, you'll see we're there."

Buck looked around the populated lot and saw the banner on the side of the building.

THE SEMINOLE PLAYHOUSE PRESENTS
JONATHON LARSON'S RENT!

"You've probably seen it before," Benjamin said coyly. He took his sunglasses off, holding them in his lap. "But I'm hoping you don't mind seeing it again, with me."

Buck saw Benjamin's eager green eyes and couldn't help but smile at his schoolboy charm. Undoing the car's belt, he leaned across the seat, kissing Benjamin's welcoming lips.

"A musical about HIV, drug addiction, and the angst of twenty-somethings," Buck jokingly said. "You do know how to set a mood on a first date, don't you?"

"Sorry, but *Sweeney Todd* ended last month," Benjamin answered. "And there aren't any meat pie shops around here."

He unfastened his seat belt, reached across, taking Buck gently by the head, and kissed him again. "I keep telling you, it's the Southern charm."

"And here I thought that was a myth," Buck whispered back. "Like the Jackalope or Bigfoot."

Benjamin sat back, letting go of Buck. He snorted with discontentment.

"You know," Benjamin said. He unlocked the car door and got out. "You can really kill a mood."

The truck door shut harder than needed. Buck remained still as Benjamin made his way around the truck's tailgate.

"Sometimes I can be a chauvinist and I don't think," Agent 98 said as he stepped down from the passenger's side. "A friend of mine jokes that my internal editor quit and won't come back without serious negotiations."

Benjamin's boyish pout changed to a smile. He looked at Buck's sincere expression. "You're so full of shit," he teased. "I'm surprised you aren't wearing adult-sized Pull-Ups."

"You assume I'm wearing any underwear at all."

"No," Benjamin said with a salacious glance at Buck's pants. "I really don't." He led the way into the theater. "I do look forward to finding out if my hypothesis is correct."

Inside the theater lobby they moved directly to the Will Call ticket line. The man behind the plastic half-partition smiled broadly as they approached.

"Now I know why you called for these tickets," said the man behind the open window. He gave the tickets to Benjamin with an obvious wink, offering Buck a knowing smile.

"That was real subtle, Patrick," Benjamin replied. A tinge of pink crept into his cheeks. "Real subtle."

"Friend of yours?" Buck said as they entered the auditorium. They walked down the theater's center aisle.

"I called in a favor," Benjamin explained. "And he arranged our seats."

They sat in the first two seats of row J.

"Please tell him 'thank you' from me," Buck said, highly impressed. "These are great!"

Buck's grin showed his full appreciation.

"I've done a few productions here," Benjamin said proudly.

"And I'm guessing they like you, Sally Field. They really, really like you." Buck paused to look at Benjamin, smiled, and spoke with sincerity. "I like you, too. Thanks for this." He gave Benjamin's leg a brief squeeze and leaned in to give him a kiss.

Benjamin pulled back and turned to intensely study his program. Buck stared at him incredulously.

"Really?" he said, shocked. "Not even in a musical theater playhouse? This is the gay version of a baroque church and you just passed up the sacrament."

Benjamin looked at him, conflicted. He opened his mouth to say something when an announcement rang through the speakers.

"Ladies and gentlemen, please take this time to use the bathroom and turn off your cell phones. The performance will start in a few minutes."

"Now, wasn't that convenient," Buck said with a smile. "If I didn't know better, I'd have sworn you planned it that way."

"Saved by the courtesy announcement," Benjamin answered with satisfaction.

"Saved by your Southern charm is more like it." Buck rolled his eyes.

The house lights went out. Benjamin's hand found Buck's leg as the first actors stomped their way onto the stage. His hand remained there until the drag queen character entered and began dancing on the table. She did a backflip off, making a perfect landing on her heels. The audience burst into applause.

"Oh my God!"

Buck snapped to attention in his seat. Benjamin's hand got knocked off, hitting the wooden divider.

"He's good!" Benjamin whispered. He nodded with enthusiasm. "And a friend of mine. I'll introduce you after—"

"No," Buck interrupted, shifting in his seat. The color ran from his face. His eyes were wide, his mouth hung slightly ajar. "I gotta go."

Benjamin's applause slowed and stopped in midair. The drag queen continued his song. Buck was already halfway out of his seat.

"What's wrong?" Benjamin asked in a frantic whisper.

"I can't explain it right now," Buck leaned over. "I just have to go."

"Shhhh!" The admonishment came from the woman behind them.

"Shush yourself!" Buck said back in a stage whisper.

He pulled out of Benjamin's grip and started a brisk walk up the aisle. He got as far as the theater's front door before he suddenly stopped, frantically patting his pants pockets.

"Forgot I drove, didn't you?"

Buck spun around to find Benjamin holding out the truck key.

"No," Buck said with a sulk. "I was reaching for my phone. Go back in, Benji. I have to go. This doesn't involve you."

"You called me Benji," he said with a stern expression. "Now I have to stay so I can kill you later."

"Look," Buck said. "You're totes adorable with all that, but I really have to go. This is literally a matter of life and death!"

He pulled out his phone and pressed the power button.

"Buck!" Benjamin reached out and grabbed hold of the phone. "Tell me what the hell is going on! Are you in some kind of trouble?"

Buck looked at him, trying to decide what to say.

"I need to get back to my car," he said. "I have to do something immediately, and time is running out."

"Fine," Benjamin said. "I'll drive you back. First you need to tell me why you ran out of there."

"I don't have time."

"It'll be faster than you calling a cab or having to walk back to my place."

Buck stared at the man, simultaneously admiring and hating his resolve. Letting his shoulders fall, he gave in with a heavy sigh.

"I can't say much right now," Buck said. "I'll explain if and when I can. But for right now, let's say I realized something very important."

"What's that?"

"Collins's Code," Buck said. He picked up his pace, starting to jog, leading Benjamin back to his car. "Now I need some kind of proof!"

"What the hell is going on?" Benjamin said. He ran ahead to catch up.

"Drop me off at my car," Buck explained. "Then I'm going to need you to find the governor and give him a message."

CHAPTER TWENTY-SEVEN

Agent 46 shimmied with great agility over the metal gate surrounding the property of UnCharted Construction's home office.

"Thank God there isn't barbed wire," she muttered, landing on the pavement on the other side.

Crouching against the metal, she spied around and saw nothing move. She glanced through the mesh to the outside world, looking for any other movement, and was happy to find not even wind stirring. Not that anything was expected in the industrial part of the city early on a Sunday afternoon.

Slowly she stood up, taking a moment to look for any signs of the van or the two men she'd seen inside. Parked down the street, Noxia had watched the passenger of the blue company truck get out and unlock the gate. The van disappeared behind the building, the man quickly pulling the metal fence closed before running after the truck.

That was ten minutes ago. Neither the men nor the truck had left the property since then.

The governor's speech should be on its way by now, Noxia thought. An impish smile curled her lips at the thought of Reverend Walker getting her message.

Agent 46 tugged on the black half jacket covering her white sleeveless shirt, and the gun resting in the left shoulder holster.

Darting over to the building, she hugged the wall, thankful for the cool brick and the slight shadow. Creeping to the edge of the building, she carefully peeked around.

The pavement from the front turned into a gravel parking lot stretching the length of the closed-up building, ending at a dirt field. Four identical company vans were parked together opposite the building's loading dock. A short walk past the gravel's end sat a grounded, run-down trailer with vinyl siding. The sun reflected powerfully off the metal door, causing a blinding, winking starburst.

"A brand-new metal door on a dilapidated storage trailer?" Noxia muttered. "That's a little odd."

Gauging the distance across to the trucks, she gave the area a quick look and took off running. Once in the safety of the blue vans' shelter, she crept toward the trailer. Something caught her eye and Noxia ducked down, pressing herself against the nose of the van. She peered out with great stealth and watched a figure approaching the shed from the loading dock.

"Angel?" Agent 46 whispered. From the yellow shirt and jeans she deduced he was the same passenger she'd seen earlier.

The foreman stopped in front of the trailer door, putting down a paper grocery bag. Fumbling with a set of keys, he opened two locks and, using his shoulder, pushed open the metal door. A dirt cloud stirred up as the door slid closed.

Scanning across the gravel, Noxia spotted the closed door of the main building. No one else was coming out. It was only a few yards to the trailer and she darted off, scurrying around the corner.

The window above her head was covered with newspapers taped over the inside. She pressed her ear against the shed's wall, but heard nothing. Agent 46 reached into her jacket, taking out her gun. Pressing against the cool vinyl siding she crept along the shed's perimeter. All the windows were covered. Noxia made her way around, hugging the side and waiting for Angel to exit the shed.

"Whoever the hell you are," said the voice from behind her, "turn around slowly and keep your hands where I can see them."

Agent 46 stood up, slowly putting her hands out by her shoulders. The gun pointed upward.

"Drop the gun to the ground," the voice commanded. "And turn around."

She did as she was told. The Beretta hit the gravel with a dull smack.

It took her a moment to recognize one of the governor's home security guards. The stout man with tousled dark hair stood a yard away, arms extended and holding a pistol pointed directly at her chest.

"Jimmy?" Agent 46 said, shocked and astonished when she saw his face.

"Mrs. Truque?" Jimmy said incredulously. "What the fuck are you doing here?"

The moment of hesitation was all she needed. Agent 46 kicked her leg up and swept it in an arc, knocking the gun from his hand. She spun around, landing on both feet with fists balled and ready to fight. Her gun lay on the ground behind her and she made a dive to reach it.

The guard moved quickly for a man of portly stature. Leaping after her, Jimmy managed to grab Noxia's leg and pull her to him. Hitting the ground sent her hand knocking into the gun handle. The Beretta was sent spinning another yard away in the dirt. Using her calves like a gym rope, Jimmy pulled her leg, climbing up her body.

Noxia managed to turn over onto her back underneath Jimmy's weight. She worked her leg up until her knee was bent enough to kick, pushing him back and off her. Rolling to her stomach, she crept forward, reaching out for the gun handle. As her fingers stretched to touch it, Jimmy grabbed hold of her ankle, pulling her back.

"Oh no you don't, you bitch," he growled at her.

"I hate being called a bitch!"

Agent 46 kicked her free leg, slamming her heel into his forehead. He let go of her ankle and fell back onto her leg. Crashing her free leg onto his chest, she knocked the wind out of him and wrapped her calves around the man's thick neck. Locking her feet around each other, she stretched out her legs and squeezed.

Jimmy began choking, trying desperately to pull her legs from his neck. His fist pounded against her muscles but she held tight.

"That hurts, you asshole," Noxia cried as Jimmy dug the blunt fingernails from his hands into her legs, raking them downward.

Agent 46 felt the guard's resistance lessen. She gave a final squeeze before kicking him away from her. Spinning around she darted forward, grabbing the discarded Beretta and rolling to a kneeling position. She aimed the gun squarely at Jimmy's forehead.

"These were good jeans, too," she said, noting the tear on her knee. A small bead of blood soaked through.

"Now," she said, "you're the one who's going to put his hands where I can see them and stand up slowly."

"I never did like you." Jimmy sneered. Reluctantly, he put his hands up and stood. "You always were an uppity bitch."

She fired the pistol, missing his foot by an inch. The silencer dulled the sound. The bullet made a thud, stirring up a small dust cloud as it shot into the ground. Immediately the gun was back aiming at his forehead.

"Say that word one more time," Agent 46 said. "I dare you."

The man stood silent, seething.

"Where's Alejandro?" she asked.

Jimmy's angry eye slits relaxed into their wider normal appearance. A smug smile transformed across his face.

"I don't know what you're talking about." He snorted his discontentment.

"Really? What's in the shed?"

"Tools," was the arrogant reply. "A tractor, maybe even a rake. Did you need a weed whacker, you ho?"

"Why don't you give me a tour?" Noxia purred back.

"Why don't you bite me?"

"If that's how you talk to a lady," Noxia said, "I'm guessing you have a grand affiliation with your game console. Slowly move around and let me in the trailer."

Jimmy's smile broadened. His arms lowered and he defiantly folded them across his chest.

"No," he said. "And fuck you."

"I don't think you're in any position to refuse me," Noxia said. She nudged the gun's muzzle in case he didn't see it aimed at him.

"And I don't think you're in any position to give orders," the voice from behind her calmly stated. "Drop the pistol and turn around with your hands up."

"What if I don't?" Agent 46 taunted without moving. "What if I decide to take a potshot at your boy here. What then?"

"I'm out a half-witted brother-in-law," the voice said. "And there's a bullet in that pretty head of yours. I don't mind making a widow of my sister. How do you feel about your skull?"

The seconds ticked off loudly inside her mind.

Her thumb slid forward, disengaging the Beretta's hammer. When she raised her arms, the gun fell to the ground for the second time. Slowly she turned around to see who had gotten the better of her.

Behind the gun pointed at her head stood a man she recognized from the photos Buck had sent her. A rounded guy with a balding head and fleshy face studied her from a set of deep-set piggish eyes. The stubble of a beard covered the lower part of his face and the first of two chins.

"Is it Marc Behr or Billy Carriway?" Agent 46 asked. "I can't remember if it's Sunday or Monday."

"Call me Marc," was his answer. He nodded to Jimmy. "And who's this?"

The security guard walked around to stand next to his brother-in-law.

"Mrs. Truque. She tutors the governor's kid," Jimmy answered. "She's supposed to be on vacation or something."

"What the hell is she doing here, then?" Marc asked. "And why is she snooping around?"

"I don't know," Jimmy said.

"So then, Mrs. Truque, is it?" Marc said. He kept the gun steadily pointed. "Why don't you tell us what the hell you're doing here?"

CHAPTER TWENTY-EIGHT

B uck remained crouched down between the front two vans in UnCharted's gravel parking lot. He climbed the gate, got around the building, and made it between the trucks without seeing a soul anywhere on the property. The vinyl-sided trailer remained still and silent, only a few yards away, without any obstruction in his path.

"This is too easy," he said to himself. "Something's not right."

Agent 98 raised his head over the van's hood, enough to see the main building. The loading dock appearing locked and quiet.

"There's not even a guard dog," Buck said. "These kinds of places always have an off-hours guard dog."

The air remained still with only the sun beating down.

Agent 98 reached into his pant leg and took out his Ruger pistol. Looking around one last time, he saw no one and darted the few short yards across to the trailer. Pressing himself against the vinyl he held his breath and listened.

Nothing.

He released his breath along with some caution, sidestepping to the door. Turning around, he noticed the hinge lock six inches above the doorknob. It was latched but not secured by a padlock. Buck placed his palms against the metal, gently pushing and testing the door's weight.

I'm not kicking this in, Buck thought.

He reached down and took hold of the knob, turning it slowly in his hand. It moved with the ease of not being locked, easily turning the 180 degrees needed to open. With his gun in hand, Buck put his shoulder against the metal door and used his strength to push it open.

The resistance was heavy. The door slid open, grinding against the earthen floor, summoning ghosts in the dirt. It reluctantly gave six inches before Buck's arms shot up through the opening, gun aimed and ready.

Sitting alone, tied to the chair against the back wall, was Alejandro, in a dirty shirt and a pair of shorts. Unkempt black hair matted around the blindfold covering the boy's eyes. Silver duct tape covered his mouth. His arms were tied in back of the chair. The boy sat slumped forward in the seat, looking like a rag doll in bondage.

"Alejandro?" Buck stage whispered into the room.

At the sound of his name the boy picked up his head. Turning it slightly to focus his blind hearing, Alejandro struggled excitedly in his chair, his arms frantically trying to move from behind. He tried to cry out. All sounds were muffled by the tape that covered his mouth.

Buck gave the door another shove and pushed his way into the room. Light filtered through the newspaper-covered windows, casting a gray tone over the shed's interior. The floor was natural dirt, hosting a bevy of miscellaneous discarded tools, scrap pieces of metal, and forgotten nails. He darted across to the boy, immediately getting on his knees.

"Alejandro," Agent 98 said. "My name is Buck and I'm a friend of your father. I'm going to get you out of here."

Putting the gun down, Buck fumbled with the ropes across the boy's waist and chest. He reached behind Alejandro's head and took off the blindfold. The sight of the boy's face caused him to pause for an instant.

Alejandro squinted in the sudden light. A pair of oval green eyes slowly opened, taking Buck into view. They studied him for any signs of familiarity before opening wide basset-hound style, the eyebrows arching back as if they were gazing at their first bag of jellybeans.

"Give me one moment," Buck said. "I'm going to try and take this tape off without hurting you."

The eyebrows fell and Alejandro's soft expression turned harder. The boy's struggling immediately ceased and he remained still as if a propped-up rag doll.

Buck eased the tape off the skin. Alejandro opened his mouth to breathe, stretching his jaw.

"Are you hurt?"

"No," the boy said sharply. "But you do know this is a trap, right?"

Buck froze in mid-motion.

"What?" he said incredulously.

"Touch that gun and I'll blow your head all over the kid," said a voice from behind him. "Keep your hands where I can see them and stand up slow."

"I told you so," Alejandro said.

"You know, kid," Buck said snidely, "you're really not helping at the moment."

"Turn around," commanded the voice.

Buck put his hands at his shoulders and, once standing, slowly turned to face his adversary.

"Angel," Buck said. "I knew it."

The foreman stood in the space behind the door and the back wall. It was the one spot Buck hadn't checked upon entering. In one hand Angel held a loop of rope. With the other, he pointed a handgun directly at Buck.

"You're not surprised?" Angel asked, walking closer. He stopped two yards away, keeping the pistol aimed at Buck's chest.

"I could tell you 525,600 reasons why I'm not surprised," Buck answered.

"I knew it!" Alejandro shouted from his chair. "I knew someone would get my clue!"

"It took me a little bit," Buck confessed. "But I figured out Collins's Code. It's from *RENT*."

Together Buck and Alejandro sang out the verse including the spelling of Angel's name.

"What the hell are you two talking about?" Angel shouted.

Buck shot his leg out and knocked the gun from Angel's hand. Spinning around he landed with both feet firmly planted on the ground. Hands curled into fists, his arm shot forward and met Angel squarely in the jaw.

Angel reeled back from the blow but recovered fast. His hands immediately balled up in front of him. He took a swing.

Buck ducked and danced backward, missing the flying fist. His arm shot out and connected into Angel's stomach. The blow caused the bigger man to double over.

Angel charged into Buck's abdomen, causing both men to fall onto the ground. They rolled away from Alejandro before Angel struggled to get on top of Buck. He sat up, raising his arm, and sent his fist crashing against the side of Buck's head.

Agent 98 bucked his hips, sending Angel tumbling off him. He darted out from underneath, scurrying to his feet. Angel rolled into a somersault and leapt to a standing position. The two men danced in a tight circle, throwing jabs at one another. Each of them was trying to inch closer to Angel's dropped gun.

Buck made a lunge toward the foreman. His shoe slipped on the pebbles in the dirt floor. The momentum of Buck's fist swinging forward threw him off balance. He tumbled backward, falling onto his side.

Seeing his opportunity, Angel dove for the gun. Grabbing hold he stood up, pointing the muzzle directly at Buck.

"Get on your knees," Angel ordered.

"Usually I wait until after a date buys me dinner," Buck replied.

"I'm not your date!" Angel snarled.

"Date. Trick. John. Clergyman. It's all the same to me," Buck said. "Either way, I still want dinner first."

"Stay there," Angel ordered. "Keep your hands behind your back."

Buck rested on his knees and the pads of his feet. He looked about for his gun but found no sign of it. Desperate for anything of use, he scanned the ground. A small plastic tube six inches long and about an inch in diameter lay less than a foot between where he was kneeling and the chair where Alejandro was tied.

He looked up and saw Alejandro staring with a single raised eyebrow and a doubtful expression. The boy was shaking his head, and his shoulders slowly moved up and down as if he were trying to keep from laughing. He tapped his bare foot in front of the chair leg.

"Don't mock me, kid," Buck said. "I'm here to save you."

"How's that going?" Alejandro asked.

"Shut up," Angel shouted. He walked a few paces farther, picking up his water bottle. The gun remained pointed at Buck.

"How'd you do it?" Buck asked. "How did you get the kid off the property?"

"Shut up," Angel commanded.

"I know it wasn't you who thought of the plan," Buck said. "It must have been...Jimmy? Or was it Marc? You're not smart enough for it."

"I said shut up!" Angel stepped over and pushed the gun against Buck's forehead. "Do you want me to shut you up instead?"

"I can tell you," Alejandro said from his chair. "I saw him when I went back to the house to get my stuff. I thought those guys were starting early. He came up behind me and put something over my mouth. *Chupa mi pito!*"

Angel turned away for a moment, pointing the gun at Alejandro. "Shut up, *cabrón!*"

When Angel looked away for a moment, Buck reached over and grabbed the plastic tube. His hands immediately went behind his back again.

"So you knocked him out, and what?" Buck asked. "Snuck him off the property in the truck?"

"Yeah," Angel said. He squinted at Buck, his anger coming to a boil. "Jimmy let me on and off the property before anyone else showed up. We stuck the little shit in a box the toilet came in, just in case anyone stopped us."

Angel began pacing.

"Now what am I going to do?" the foreman muttered. "This has gone too far."

Buck sat back on his heels. His hands stretched out, letting his fingers drag in the dirt behind him. Digging into the shed's floor he found a nail about an inch in length. His nimble fingers plucked it from the ground and his empty hand curled around the metal.

"You could always let us walk out of here," Buck said. "I'll be sure to put in a good word for you with my friends at the maximum security prison in Starke. That's where they executed Ted Bundy, you know."

"Shut up!" Angel commanded. He paced a few steps in each direction. *"Mierda!"*

Buck bounced the nail in his hand to gauge the weight. Behind his back, he put the nail inside the tube. Agent 98 began his breathing exercise, taking slow, deep breaths.

"They stuck him in the chair and turned on the juice," Buck taunted. His chest held more air with each breath. "Bundy fries and a shake, the two-dollar special!"

"Shut up, *chingado!*"

"Hey, Angel," Buck shouted.

Angel looked up, surprised to hear his name. Buck's hand jumped to his mouth. He took a large breath and puckered, positioning his lips against the plastic tube. With a large, sharp puff Buck let go, blowing into the tunnel.

The nail rattled through the cylinder and shot out. It flew less than a yard before falling to the ground. The room was silent as all eyes watched the horrible failure.

"What the hell was that?" Angel asked in complete disbelief.

"Really?" Alejandro called out. "Did you think that would work?"

"You know what, kid," Buck said. His head snapped around to his left shoulder to stare directly at the boy. "You're really working my last nerve here! At least I made an effort."

"Not even an A for effort," Alejandro said.

"Shut up, the both of you," Angel yelled.

Angel kept the gun pointed at Buck, turning away from Alejandro. He looked around the room, trying to find an idea.

"I can't let you go now," Angel moaned. "I'm not going to jail."

"No," Buck said. "You're too pretty. That little dance-card butt of yours will be punched every night."

Angel stared at Buck. All of his anger and frustration was concentrated on Agent 98's face. Angel's arm jutted out. He waved the pistol in Buck's direction.

"I should shoot you right now," Angel said. His breathing came fast as panic settled. "Get rid of you and the kid and get the hell out of here."

"I don't think so," Alejandro said calmly.

The boy pulled his hands free from behind his back. Reaching under the chair he grabbed Buck's gun, took quick and careful aim, and fired the Ruger before either of the adults knew what happened.

The bullet shot through Angel's hand and out the vinyl siding of the shed. The force knocked the gun from his hand, sending it sailing into the air. Angel flew backward, crashing into the wall, howling in pain.

Buck uncovered his head and picked himself up from the

dirt. He saw Angel's discarded gun a yard away and made a leap for it. He took hold of the pistol, pointing it at the wounded man on the floor. Angel clutched his hand in agony.

Greatly astonished, Buck turned to look at Alejandro. The boy stood with his legs firmly planted. Both arms were out in front of him, the gun held firmly in his small hands.

"You know how to shoot a gun?" Buck asked incredulously.

Alejandro remained in perfect stance. Only his head turned slightly to give Buck a disparaging look.

"I'm an effeminate fourteen-year-old, with a gay dad, living in the South," the boy answered bluntly. "Of course I know how to shoot a gun."

"All right then," Buck said. He was taken by surprise and still in slight shock. Angel's cries brought him out of it. "How did you get your hands untied?"

"I've been working the plastic tie against a nail in the wall," Alejandro said.

"Smart kid," Buck said. He ignored Alejandro's sharp look. "Good job."

Alejandro lowered the pistol and walked over, looking down at Angel, who still held his hand as he cried out.

"Through the hand like Holy Jesus," the boy mocked.

"Yeah," Buck said hesitantly, unnerved by the boy's shocking calm. "Now give that to me before someone else gets hurt."

Alejandro curled his lip into a sneer and snorted. "You mean like you?"

"Hand it over, young man," Buck demanded. He put his hand out for the gun. Reluctantly, Alejandro complied.

"Your father is going to be very happy to see you," Buck said. "You ready to go home?"

"Definitely," Alejandro said.

The boy lifted his head, looking into Buck's face. The green eyes held so much fear, slowly releasing it and pooling up with tears. Alejandro leapt forward, throwing his arms around

Buck and holding tight. The dam broke and the boy sobbed uncontrollably.

Agent 98 stood perfectly still, not knowing what to do. His arms were held up with a gun in each hand and the boy wrapped tightly around him. For the briefest instant Buck smiled, feeling the love and relief flowing into him from the vise grip around his waist. In another flash the smile was erased by a heavy cough, and Buck tapped the boy on the back of his shoulder.

"Alejandro," Buck said gently. "We need to get going. You're going to have to let go of me."

Alejandro raised his head. His face was wet with tears and his nose was running. The boy sniffed, blinking several times, straightening himself.

"Thank you," he whispered.

Buck looked down at the teenager. There was a familiarity about the kid that Buck couldn't identify. The sincerity in the boy's voice was the greatest thanks he had ever received. It was the sheer magnitude of the boy's earnestness that allowed Buck to overlook the snot and tear stains on his coral-colored Alfani shirt.

"Since you can obviously handle yourself," Buck said, "hold one of these guns while I get the door. It's rather heavy, if memory serves correctly."

"And it does!" they said simultaneously.

Buck turned his head and stared at the boy with new insight. He studied the boy's green oval eyes and smiled. Alejandro was definitely his father's son with his complexion and hair color, but there was something about the boy's eyes that brought a mischievous grin to Buck's lips.

"What?" Alejandro argued. "I'm strong enough to get the door."

"Let me get it," Buck said. "You stand aside. We're going home."

Agent 98 cautiously handed Alejandro a gun. With a look at

the whimpering Angel clutching his bleeding hand in the corner, Buck put his hand on the door and gave it a strong pull.

The door opened sluggishly. Agent 98 stepped back, putting his foot in front of the door and using his weight to hold it open for Alejandro.

"Don't stand there, kid," Buck chided. "Go on and get out."

"I can't," Alejandro said quietly. His hand fell to his side and he dropped the gun. "There's something blocking my way."

Buck looked at the boy standing rigid in place, starting to tremble.

"What's stopping you?" He poked his head out and looked through the open door.

Marc Behr stood less than two yards away. His piggish eyes glared and a sneer twisted his fleshy lips. He held a Beretta in his hand, pointing to his left.

Standing next to him was Agent 46, Noxia von Tüssëll, the Beretta poking into her ribs.

Alejandro found his voice.

"A fat man and Mrs. Truque are blocking my way."

CHAPTER TWENTY-NINE

S o the kid got the gun away from you, eh?" Marc said. "Says a lot."

"What are you doing with a gun, Alejandro?" Mrs. Truque scolded the boy from where she stood. She looked at Buck. "And what the hell are you doing letting a fourteen-year-old kid handle a gun?"

"I'm not a kid!" Alejandro protested.

"Shut up, all of you," Marc yelled. "Or I'll put a bullet into this one's stomach. Good. Now go stand behind your friend holding the door."

He nudged Mrs. Truque into the shed.

"Now," the fat man said. He motioned to Buck with his chin. "Let go of the door, drop the gun, and put your hands in the air where I can see them."

The door slid closed, casting them into light gray shadows.

"I heard a gunshot," Marc said. "Who fired it?"

"Marc," Angel cried from the center of the trailer. The wounded man pulled himself up to his knees before collapsing back on his heels. He clutched his bleeding hand to his chest. "I'm shot. I need help."

Marc slowly bent down and retrieved the Ruger. He walked backward, keeping his eyes and the gun pointing at the other three. Carefully, he squatted down to pick up the gun that Angel had dropped. He put Angel's gun in the back of his pants and the Ruger in the front, the gun handles sticking out of the waistband.

"I've been shot," Angel cried. His chest rose and fell with sobs. "I need help."

"Shut up, Angel," Marc replied. "I need to think."

"Marc!" Angel wailed. "I need something to stop the bleeding. I need a doctor."

"What's the plan, Marc?" Buck asked. "What are you going to do now? Keep us all hostage?"

"If that's what it takes," Marc answered.

"I need to get to a doctor," Angel begged. "Help me, Marc."

"Shut up," the heavy man cried. He ran a hand over his bald head. The yellow boat on his company shirt bobbed with each breath.

Angel remained crouched on his knees, grasping his hand in sheer agony. Blood ran out from between the fingers of his good hand, covering both of them in thick, visceral red.

"Marc." Angel looked up at his brother-in-law. "We need to go to a doctor. I need—"

The gunshot echoed loudly inside the shed, causing a sound like thunder. Angel's body jumped, thrown back against the wall by the force of the shot. He remained upright for a moment— motionless, a stunned expression cemented on his face—before falling down into the dirt.

"A spic who can't work," Marc sneered. "Twice as useless."

"I can't breathe," Alejandro complained. His face was pushed into Mrs. Truque's side to keep him from observing the murder.

"I don't want to hear a sound from any of you," Marc quietly commanded. "Here's what's going to happen. You." He motioned the pistol at Buck. "You're going to open the door and hold it open. I'm going to back out with my gun pointed at this little shit's head. Mrs. Truque or Noxia or whoever you are is going to come out next. Then you're going to come out last, letting the door close behind you. Got it?"

"Who's Noxia?" Alejandro asked, immediately picking up on the name.

"A nickname from long ago," she said with a sharp look over her shoulder, immediately dismissing his question.

"Then what'll happen?" Buck asked.

"We're going to go for a little ride," Marc said. "Georgia. Maybe Alabama or Louisiana."

"And the minute we cross state lines with the boy in tow," Mrs. Truque said, "it becomes a felony kidnapping. Thanks to the Lindbergh Law, you'll be on the FBI Most Wanted list."

"If he lives that long," Marc answered, "I'll worry about it."

"Let him go, Behr," Buck said. "You have the both of us. You don't need Alejandro. Why not let him go?"

"He's my golden ticket," Marc answered. "Once I get rid of the two of you, I'll use the kid as a bargaining chip. The door. Now."

Buck gave in with a heavy sigh and pulled the door. Using his body, he held it open while Marc and Alejandro backed out. Noxia went next and Buck followed, leaving Angel's dead body inside.

"You two," Marc ordered. "Up front and hold hands so I can see them."

"Doesn't the cliché have us putting them on our heads?" Buck asked.

"Only if we want to draw attention," Marc said. "Do it!"

Noxia and Buck did as they were told.

"You could have at least wiped your sweaty palm off," Buck whispered.

"Do you realize you have a knack for picking the exact wrong moment to start an argument?" she hissed back.

"As a matter of fact," he answered, "yes. It's a gift from God."

"Now move!" Marc ordered.

"You haven't told us where to go, butt munch," Buck chided.

"And we're going to die," Noxia said with a sigh.

"The parking lot up front," Marc answered.

They started off, Noxia and Buck holding hands. Alejandro followed a large pace behind with Marc's hand tightly gripping the nape of his neck. The gun pushed against his spine.

"You don't want to take your van," Buck said, offering friendly advice.

"Open the gate, it's unlocked," Marc commanded. "Why not?"

Buck pushed the metal barricade back on its wheels as casually as if he were doing a daily chore.

"Obvious, isn't it?" Agent 98 answered with a shrug. "They'll be looking for it."

"Who will?" Marc asked. A smug smile crossed his lips. "No one knows I have the boy. People think she's somewhere in Europe and no one gives a shit about you."

"He's got you on that one, Buck," Noxia added. "Nobody really does give a shit about you. You tend to rub people the wrong way."

"Think about it," Buck said, ignoring the comment. "You just shot a man! It's going to be a hot day, and this is Florida! How long do you think before that body starts to stink and the police put it together? Every cop from Sarasota to Seattle will be looking for a blue van with a yellow-stenciled boat and matching letters reading 'UnCharted Construction.' It's easy to spot."

"Oh my God," Noxia added with a mocking laugh. "Your entire plan was figured out by a female school tutor and a flaming queen antique dealer."

"Was that really necessary, Noxia?" Buck asked.

"You have a point," Marc said.

"And we can't all fit into her Miata," Buck continued. "There's barely enough room for her with those giraffe legs."

"I guess I had that coming," Noxia muttered.

"We'll have to take my car. The Honda over there."

"Fine," Marc said. "You drive. The bitch can sit with the kid in the back."

"Oh no you didn't!" Buck chided. "She hates being called a bitch."

"I really do," Noxia said, a chill in her voice. "Somehow, I'm going to make you pay."

"If you really want to make him pay," Buck said with a tight grin, reaching for the door's handle, "you should make him some of your muffin specials. I assure you that will get the job done."

Buck gave her a wink and got into the car.

The car doors slammed shut as the occupants settled into their seats. Marc held the gun across his lap, alternatingly pointing it at Buck behind the steering wheel and at Alejandro sitting immediately behind him.

"Make sure the two of you are buckled in back there," Marc said. "I want to see you pull on those belts to make sure. I wouldn't want anything to happen to you."

"I bet," Noxia said.

Satisfied, Marc sat back in his seat, holding the gun steady, pointed at Buck.

"Get to I-10," Marc commanded. "Go west."

"Sounds like a Village People music cue to me," Buck said.

"Who are the Village People?" Alejandro asked.

"You'll find out soon enough," Buck answered. He started to hum the song.

Agent 98 turned the engine on and the car moved out of the lot. They were halfway down the street when a police car pulled out behind them.

"Don't draw any attention to us," Marc warned, "any of you, if you know what's good for the boy."

Buck made a turn and followed the signs toward the interstate. The police car continued forward.

"Why do it?" Buck asked. "Why go through all the trouble and risk of kidnapping? It can't all be because you're an ignorant, prejudicial piece of human garbage."

"I'd watch what I say if I were you," Marc advised. "Blood will stain that pretty pink shirt of yours."

"It's coral, thank you." Buck let out an exasperated breath. "Don't any of you know your colors?"

"That really isn't pink," Alejandro said from the backseat.

"Stay out of this," Noxia said to the boy. "Buck, do you mind?"

"Besides, you're not going to shoot me. You're only holding the gun for scare tactics."

"Buck," Noxia sang out playfully from the backseat. "Didn't you see what happened to Angel? We've been through this before: Provoking the man with the gun is bad. Bad Buck, bad!"

"Come on, Noxia," Buck chided. "If he was going to shoot us, he'd have shot us. Really! Why take all of us in the car? It would have been easier to shoot both of us back there with Angel. You could have taken the kid and gone without hassles."

"Aaaannnnnd we're going to die," Noxia announced.

Buck increased the car's speed, running a stop sign. A waiting car horn echoed after him.

"That was a stop sign," Marc said. "I told you to be cool!"

"See, Noxia," Buck said, gazing into the rearview mirror. "I did what I wanted and he still didn't shoot me."

"If you don't stop acting like a complete asshole," Noxia said, "I'll grab the gun and shoot you myself!"

"I'd listen to your girlfriend in the backseat," Marc said. "The entrance ramp should be coming up here on the right. Now be real subtle like, and get onto the interstate."

"Subtle?" Buck said with a laugh.

"Oh God," Noxia moaned in the backseat. "Now we really *are* going to die."

"I'm as subtle as the Chicago Fire!" Buck declared.

"And you flame brighter!" Noxia added.

Buck turned onto the highway ramp, flooring the gas pedal. The car jerked forward, rapidly picking up speed.

"This car don't move like a Honda," Marc said.

"I've had some special work done on it," Buck confided.

"You're in for a treat." He gazed into the rearview mirror, meeting Noxia's warning glare. "Get over it!"

A joker's grin spread across the lower half of his face. His eyes grew wide and he let out a maniacal laugh.

"Fasten your seat belts," Buck ordered in his best Bette Davis impersonation. "It's going to be a bumpy ride!"

The small, dark blue car burst into traffic, quickly merging into the busy stream and cutting across to the center of the three-lane highway. The engine raced as the digital speedometer rapidly counted higher. Reaching a speed of sixty-five miles per hour, the car dashed into the farthest lane.

"Buck," Noxia said, "a little caution, please. There's two of us back here that don't wish to die."

"Have some confidence in me, will you?"

"At this point, Buck," Noxia called out, "I'd have more confidence if Helen Keller was driving!"

"Awww." Buck pouted. "That was just mean."

The dashboard registered seventy-five miles per hour. Buck cut the wheel and the car shot back into the right lane, shaking the passengers in their seats. He ignored the sounds of the honking horns.

"What the fuck do you think you're doing?" Marc said. "I told you to be inconspicuous."

"Why?" Buck asked calmly. His eyes were wide with a crazed glint, and the grin turned into a grimace, but his tone was even keeled as if he were reciting poetry. "You're going to kill us anyway. So why bother doing what you say?"

"I'll blow your fucking head off!" Marc yelled.

"No! That's precisely it! I don't think you will!" Agent 98 let out some crazed howling laughter. "If you shoot me I lose complete control of the wheel. I'll fall over and this car does more doughnuts than you'll find at a police chief's morning meeting. And we'll all go together when we go!" He gleefully sang the last line.

Buck cut into the next lane, weaving the car between a large pickup truck with bigger-than-average tires and two side-by-side motorcyclists. The bikers tooted their horns as they split into separate lanes, both flipping him the bird. Buck only screamed with cartoonish laughter.

"That was fun, wasn't it?" Agent 98 reached over for the switch to flash his lights at the car in front of him. A digital outline of the car appeared in the GPS screen's corner. He started whistling the tune "Do You Know the Muffin Man."

Marc turned the gun to the backseat, aiming it at Alejandro. "I'll kill the kid!" he taunted. "You want to laugh at that?"

"Buck," Noxia warned from the backseat. "Do us all a favor and listen to the man with the gun."

"Kill him," Buck stated calmly, "and I slam this car into the divider wall and we all go up in flames. Either way, you're just as dead as we are. Choose your own adventure!"

Buck flashed his lights at the car in front of him. Letting out another bout of crazed laughter, he leaned into the gas pedal. The digital numbers raced above eighty miles per hour. The souped-up Civic wildly changed lanes, rapidly swerving between cars.

Other cars on the highway moved out of his way. The ones that didn't, Buck swerved around at lightning speed. As he came upon a Prius he flashed his lights in warning. The driver in front defiantly hit the brakes—both tail lights flashing red.

Given no warning, and at the speed he was going, Buck tried to swerve the car to avoid hitting the Prius. The front end of the Civic clipped the plastic bumper of the Toyota, ripping it from the vehicle as the blue car flew by.

Car horns sounded like a full-orchestrated symphony from every direction.

Buck glanced in the rearview and saw Alejandro pulled against Noxia in the backseat.

"Get off," Marc said.

"Not without dinner and a movie," Buck answered. "Oh, you mean at the exit. Sure."

With a sharp turn of the wheel the car switched lanes, cutting off a semi. The truck's baritone horn echoed down the highway.

"This isn't funny," Noxia called out. "Don't!"

"Perfect suggestion," Buck cried in glee. Changing lanes abruptly he belted out "Don't Rain on My Parade" from the musical *Funny Girl*.

"Doesn't Audra McDonald sing that?" Alejandro asked from the backseat.

Buck looked into the rearview and saw the boy pulled into Noxia's protection.

"I *love* me some Audra McDonald!" Buck yelped.

"Oh God," Noxia cried. "They've bonded."

"Take the next exit," Marc said, the gun pointed at Buck. Sweat beaded on the fleshy skin's surface, and his tiny, round eyes registered fear.

"This exit?"

The car was approaching the exit ramp at eighty miles per hour when Buck made the turn at the last minute. The Honda rode over the outlined median, flying down the paved road. The ramp curved around with a guardrail lining both sides and a grassy field stretching to the right.

"Buck," Noxia screamed, bracing herself against the door. Her fingers wrapped around the locked handle. "You're going to get us killed!"

"I'm sick of your complaining, Noxia," Buck said. "Get out!"

Agent 98 gave the wheel a sharp turn, sending the car up on its right side, balancing on two wheels. The roof of the car scraped along the guardrail, sending sparks flying. Marc crashed into the car door, his gun hand braced against the roof. Alejandro was thrown into Noxia, pressing her against the passenger door in the back.

The car fell back onto all four wheels, bouncing the inside passengers like a shaken snow globe. The car was motionless for an instant while everyone inside remained still with shock. The tires spun in place and the Civic lurched forward.

The dashboard showed the numbers rapidly climbing at thirty-five miles per hour when Buck hit the door's control panel, opening the car's rear passenger door.

Noxia tugged on the handle. She grabbed Alejandro by the collar of his torn and dirty T-shirt and pulled hard, and they both tumbled out of the moving vehicle. They rolled onto the grass and away from the road.

Buck looked at the terrified man in the passenger seat. Dirt powdered his face, causing creases in the perspiration beading his skin. The gun was still in his hand, but the hand was pressed against the roof as Marc tried to regain his balance.

"It's just you and me, sweetheart!"

Agent 98's foot hit the gas pedal. The Civic rattled and sped off. He ignored the stop sign at the end of the exit ramp and cut the wheel, making a sharp right turn.

Marc was thrown to the left, his body shifting in the seat belt. Buck's left fist crossed over and pounded Marc in the face. Marc dropped the gun onto the car floor. The seat belt pulled him back into the passenger seat. As he made a lunge to retrieve the pistol, Buck hit the brakes.

The car skidded, causing the seat belt to lock and restrain Marc in his seat. Rubber burned and smoke marked the spot on the road as the car shot forward. Buck reached over, throwing another punch.

Marc grabbed Buck's arm and began twisting his fist. The car swerved, cutting across the lane dividers. It ran a red light, causing the approaching SUV to slam on its brakes, sending it into a tailspin.

The Civic gained speed down a long stretch of road. Intersecting streets were random and the area wasn't heavily residential. The car raced along at fifty, sixty, and up to seventy miles per hour when Marc's voice broke the silence.

"Game over," Marc said. Angel's gun was back in his hand,

pointing at Buck. "Stop the car or I'll shoot you, and I don't give a damn what happens!"

Buck flashed his lights. The digital car outline appeared on the GPS screen. The red "X" appeared and locked onto position.

"Done."

Buck slammed his foot on the brake pedal while pulling the emergency brake. The car's wheels locked, stopping suddenly on the pavement. A loud screeching echoed as friction burned the tires and smoke surrounded the car. Buck's seat belt held in place. As the driver's emergency air bag immediately inflated, Agent 98 heard the scream and the glass shattering as Marc went through the windshield.

CHAPTER THIRTY

W ell, I'm packed and ready to go," Buck announced as he entered the kitchen. He wore a pair of Confederate gray slacks and a port-colored shirt. The smell of brewed coffee and the sound of low conversation met him at once.

"And that is reason for an announcement?" Phynilla asked. She was leaning against the kitchen counter, holding a ceramic mug to her lips.

"How else to let the common people know?" Buck answered. He moved next to her and poured the last cup from the coffeepot.

"There are many things I may be, Mr. Miller," Phynilla said, her head weaving on her shoulders, "but common is not among them. Oh Kay?"

Her painted candy-apple lips curved into a smile.

"I'm sorry to hear about your brother," Buck said. "I know that's kind of ironic coming from me."

"Not really," Phynilla disparagingly said. "CJ has been dealing with his demons for most of his life. Some I knew about, and some I didn't. Either way he's my brother and I love him. Now that he's skipped town along with the church's money, I'm guessing he's gonna have himself a whole new bunch of reasons to be lookin' over his shoulder."

"Maybe the Pilgrim's Church will take you back as pastor?" Buck suggested.

"They offered," Phynilla said. "But I declined. Being pastor is like being married to the church, and we divorced for a reason. I have no ill will toward the Pilgrim's Church of the Holy Trinity, but it's best we don't see each other for a while. Sooner or later I'll learn to love again, if you get my meaning?"

"I think I do," Buck said quietly. He put his hand out to her. "I wish you the best."

The light blue shadow showed on her lids as she slowly scanned downward.

"You too," she simply replied.

Phynilla Jackson gave Buck a brief smile and raised her coffee mug in salute before turning and walking out of the kitchen, leaving him with his hand extended.

"I'll be in your office if you need me, Governor," she called over her shoulder. "I have a lot of work to do."

"I really hope I haven't offended her too badly," Buck said, sitting at the kitchen table.

"She'll be fine," Miguel said.

"Besides," Noxia said. "That's a warm reception compared to the one I got."

"She's upset," Miguel said. "And for good reasons. But she also knows it wasn't either of your fault. She'll come around, eventually."

"And what about you?" Buck asked.

"There's less than two months until the election," Governor Reyes said. "I'll continue to push R-65, but reelection isn't as important to me anymore. It's up to the people of Florida now. I'm taking the rest of this week off, though. I need to spend time with Alejandro. Buck…"

Miguel's brown eyes brimmed with tears. He clenched his jaw to keep it from trembling and blinked his eyes.

"Thank you doesn't seem enough…"

"It's enough for me," Buck said. "That, and getting R-65 passed."

"I thought you didn't want a husband," Miguel said with a grin.

"I wouldn't mind having a husband," Buck playfully answered. "Just not one of my own."

"Papi!" Alejandro came bursting into the room. He was dressed in a pair of swim shorts and a T-shirt. A towel was draped over his shoulders. "Are you ready yet?"

"Give me five minutes," Miguel said. He scooted his chair out from the table to give his son a big hug. "Let me go get changed and we can take the boat out."

Miguel smiled down at his son. He hugged the boy close for several long minutes. Closing his eyes he took a few deep breaths, most likely trying to let go of how close to danger his family had journeyed. He lifted Alejandro's face by the chin and looked down, studying his son. Miguel started for his bedroom, playfully swatting Alejandro on the butt as he left.

"Buck," Alejandro said.

"Mr. Miller." Noxia immediately corrected the boy.

"It's okay," Agent 98 said. "You can call me Buck. After everything we've been through, I think we're beyond that formality."

Alejandro's face lit up. "Buck," he said, grinning with pride. "Can I talk to you for a moment?"

"Sure."

Alejandro turned and gave Noxia a direct stare.

"Oh," she clumsily said. She stood from the table. "I can take a hint. I'll go get changed and meet you boys back here."

As soon as they were alone, Alejandro sat at the table. He motioned for Buck to sit across from him.

"I want to say thanks." Alejandro stumbled through the words. "You saved my life. You're kind of my hero."

Buck smiled, a flush of crimson creeping into his cheeks. He sat back in the chair, puffed at the chest. "I wouldn't say hero," he said with false modesty.

"I would," Alejandro said.

"You're very welcome," Buck said. He was about to stand when he noticed that Alejandro hadn't moved. "Is there something else?"

"Well," the boy shyly confessed, "yeah. My dad is taking me to New York City before school starts again. And we're going to see a musical on Broadway."

"That's wonderful," Buck said. "Tell me which one and I'll get you the CD. It'll be a present from me."

"I was hoping," Alejandro said, his eyes focused on the center of the table, "that you might want to come with us? I know Papi wouldn't mind."

The boy lifted his head and looked Buck directly in the eyes. Alejandro resembled his father so much, except for his eyes, those almond-shaped green eyes that held so much hope and complete fear all at once.

Buck's breath stopped as the full meaning of the boy's invitation dawned on him. He took an extra moment knowing that he would have to be very careful in how he answered.

"I'm sorry," Buck said with a sincere smile. "I can't. I'm going home to the West Coast and I'll have to go back to work."

"There's no way you can put it off for a little bit?" Alejandro asked. His voice was soft and cracked with anxiety. "Not even if I said please?"

"I would like to," Buck said, smiling. "But I can't."

"Can't what?" Benjamin asked.

He came in wearing a pair of blue jeans and a red button-down shirt. The collar was open, revealing chest hair, and a pair of dark sunglasses rested on top of his disheveled sun-bleached hair.

"Stay for the next production at the Playhouse," Buck answered quickly.

Alejandro smiled, showing his gratitude for keeping his secret.

"The next one is *Gypsy*," Benjamin said. "Do you have that one?"

"I have eight different CDs of *Gypsy*," Buck said.

"Why does anyone need eight different versions of *Gypsy*?" Miguel said, coming back into the kitchen. He was dressed in an orange shirt with black shorts and a pair of sandals. Noxia was directly behind him.

"Which one is the best?" Alejandro asked.

The answers came at once.

"Patti LuPone," Benjamin said.

"Angela Lansbury," Buck answered.

"Bernadette Peters," Miguel replied.

"Didn't Bette Midler do a version of that musical?" Noxia asked.

All three of the men simultaneously turned to stare at her audacity. Then they burst out laughing at her answer.

"Come on, *m'ijito*," Miguel said. "Let's go make sure we have everything."

He reached over, picking Alejandro up. He threw the boy over his shoulder and carried him from the room.

"Are you ready to go?" Benjamin asked once the laughter subsided.

"Yeah, but don't you have to work?" Buck asked.

"Not anymore," Benjamin said with a sheepish grin. "You're talking to one of the unemployed masses."

"What happened?"

"I couldn't work there anymore," Benjamin confessed. "It's one thing to make snide comments privately, but it's another to kidnap the governor's son. I don't need to be associated with any kind of homophobic company like that."

"I'm sorry," Buck said.

"Look at it this way," Benjamin replied with a smile. "I'm free to take you to the airport. And I have no plans for the next couple of weeks. Those your Rimowa bags at the front door?"

Buck's grin was uncontrollable. "They definitely are. And extra points for recognizing the luggage."

"Please!" Benjamin said. "I know style when I see it. I recognized you in a dark bar. I'll just grab these for you and give you a chance to finish saying good-bye."

"Thanks," Buck said. "Maybe we can talk about a few travel options to fill your time."

"As long as you can suggest a good travel buddy to go along," Benjamin said. He leaned in and gave Buck a gentle kiss on the lips.

"I guess this means you're out at work now?"

"I'm not at work anymore." Benjamin smiled. "I'll meet you at the truck."

He took off for the front door, leaving Buck alone with Noxia.

"That one will get you in trouble," Noxia said.

"Yeah," Buck answered. "I could use a little trouble about now."

Noxia turned to face him with a smirk. "You are such a delicate flower."

They watched Benjamin pulling the luggage across the lawn. The costumed dogs barked for a brief moment when he passed the countess sleeping under a lawn umbrella, the rifle propped against her shoulder in military fashion.

"Alejandro's a good kid," Buck said to Noxia. "As far as kids go. You did a good job."

"I don't know how much credit I can take as a summer tutor," Noxia said. Her pride was evident by the way her face lit up at the boy's mention.

"You know your son is gay, don't you?" Buck asked.

Noxia faced him with a flabbergasted look. Her olive-tinted skin took on a pinkish hue and her mouth opened in surprise. She stuttered without saying a word and choked on nervous laughter.

"Why is everyone a closet case with you?" Noxia said. "There's no way to tell at fourteen years of age."

"Believe me," Buck said, breaking out into a full grin, "there are ways to tell. He just asked me to join them in New York. I'm pretty sure he was hoping for a date."

"He means it as a friend." Noxia dismissed the comment, laughing. "He has a bad case of hero worship. Think about it. You rescued him from being kidnapped. Of course he has a boy crush on you."

"I saved *your* boy from being kidnapped," Buck insisted, getting back to the main subject. "Don't avoid the point."

"Come on, Buck," Noxia said forcing another laugh. "You know that…"

She saw his fixed expression and knew she'd lost the argument.

"Alejandro can never know," she whispered fiercely.

"I knew it!" Agent 98 said with triumph.

"How did you figure it out?"

"I've known you for many years," Buck said. "I've seen your emerald eyes sparkle, glare, attack, signal, reveal secrets, shoot daggers, and roll at my sarcasm more often than I care to think about. I'd know those green acidic pools anywhere. Alejandro has the only other set I've ever seen."

"I mean it, Buck," Noxia warned. "No one can know."

"How?" Buck stammered. "I mean really, Noxia von Tüssëll, a mother?"

"Miguel wanted to be a parent," Agent 46 explained. "I didn't. Adoption wasn't an option for him at the time."

"That's one huge favor to ask," Buck said.

"I have no regrets," Noxia answered. "He's a great father, and let's face it, I'm not exactly the maternal type. He only asked that we never tell Alejandro the truth. The boy thinks his mother is dead, so there's no reason to ever tell him."

"And you don't mind?"

"Miguel was kind enough to make an amendment, offering to let me be a part of his life," Noxia said with a smile. "And Mrs. Truque was born."

"You're an amazing person, Miss Barbe Noxia von Tüssëll Truque," Buck said with rare sincerity. "I truly admire you."

"Thank you, Buck," Noxia said. She put a hand on his shoulder. "That's probably one of the nicest things you've ever said to me."

"And your son is going to grow up to be a big homo."

"You can't know that now," Noxia protested.

"Parents are always the last to see the obvious."

"I think I'm a little more in tune with my gaydar than most mothers," Noxia said.

"Please," Buck said. "You're Isis, mother of denial. The facts are so clear!"

"Buck," Noxia protested.

The sounds of barking came from the front yard, immediately followed by two rifle blasts. At the sound of the gunshots Miguel and Alejandro came running back inside.

"What was that?" Miguel said.

"It came from out front!" Alejandro took off running.

"M'ijito," Miguel called out. "Wait!"

Alejandro ran out the front door followed by Noxia, Buck, and Miguel. They stood on the front porch in complete shock, not knowing what to do.

The two dogs dressed as a lion and a tiger were under the lawn chair, peeking out and barking wildly. The countess was standing up, aiming the rifle into the sky. Bracing it against her shoulder, she pulled the trigger and was knocked back down from the blast.

Countess Margareta Theresa Valois Stewart Rosenblatt jumped back up as if she were an inflatable clown. She threw the rifle onto the ground and started running across the lawn. Her arms flailed wildly as she jumped and pointed to the sky.

"Jenny! Bring that bitch back," she cried, running down the hill. "Jenny! Jeeeennnnyyyyyyyyy!"

Buck followed the pointing finger, looking up into the cloudless sky.

A large eagle was circling above, carrying something in its talons that let out pitiful cries.

"Well," Alejandro declared breathily. Resting all of his weight on his back leg, he placed both hands on his hips. "I'm guessing that dog was serving some rabbit realness!"

The boy took off running after the countess. Governor Reyes quickly ran after him.

Buck remained perfectly still. He turned his head as if in slow motion, looking directly at Noxia, his eyebrows pointedly arched and a smug smile stuck on his lips.

"Okay," she conceded under her breath. "Maybe we know."

She shook her head at him, accepting his growing smile in return. They both took off running across the lawn. There was a final yelp before the eagle, clasping tightly to its prey, disappeared over the treetops.

About the Author

Eric Andrews-Katz was born in New York. When he was twelve years of age, his family moved to Florida without asking him. Eventually, he studied creative writing at USF before attending the Florida School of Massage. Since moving to Seattle in 1994, Eric has a successful licensed massage business (The Massage Guy™) and lives with his partner, Alan. Eric's work can be found in these anthologies: *So Fey: Queer Fairy Fiction*, *The Best Date Ever*, *Charmed Lives: Gay Spirit in Storytelling* (a Lambda Literary Award finalist), *Gay City*: Volumes 2, 3, and 4 (which he also co-edited), and *Zombiality: A Queer Bent on the Undead*. Eric is also a contributing writer for the *Seattle Gay News*. He can be found at: www.EricAndrewsKatz.com or reached at WriteOn530@gmail.com.

Books Available From Bold Strokes Books

Café Eisenhower by Richard Natale. A grieving young man who travels to Eastern Europe to claim an inheritance finds friendship, romance, and betrayal, as well as a moving document relating a secret lifelong love affair. (978-1-62639-217-5)

Balls & Chain by Eric Andrews-Katz. In protest of the marriage equality bill, the son of Florida's governor has been kidnapped. Agent Buck 98 is back, and the alligators aren't the only things biting. (978-1-62639-218-2)

Murder in the Arts District by Greg Herren. An investigation into a new and possibly shady art gallery in New Orleans' fabled Arts District soon leads Chanse into a dangerous world of forgery, theft...and murder. A Chanse MacLeod mystery. (978-1-62639-206-9)

Rise of the Thing Down Below by Daniel W. Kelly. Nothing kills sex on the beach like a fishman out of water...Third in the Comfort Cove Series. (978-1-62639-207-6)

Calvin's Head by David Swatling. Jason Dekker and his dog, Calvin, are homeless in Amsterdam when they stumble on the victim of a grisly murder—and become targets for the calculating killer, Gadget. (978-1-62639-193-2)

The Return of Jake Slater by Zavo. Jake Slater mistakenly believes his lover, Ben Masters, is dead. Now a wanted man in Abilene, Jake rides to Mexico to begin a new life and heal his broken heart. (978-1-62639-194-9)

Backstrokes by Dylan Madrid. When pianist Crawford Paul meets lifeguard Armando Leon, he accepts Armando's offer to help him overcome his fear of water by way of private lessons. As friendship turns into a summer affair, their lust for one another turns to love. (978-1-62639-069-0)

The Raptures of Time by David Holly. Mack Frost and his friends journey across an alien realm, through homoerotic adventures, suffering humiliation and rapture, making friends and enemies, always seeking a gateway back home to Oregon. (978-1-62639-068-3)

The Thief Taker by William Holden. Unreliable lovers, twisted family secrets, and too many dead bodies wait for Thomas Newton in London—where he soon discovers that all the plotting is aimed directly at him. (978-1-62639-054-6)

Waiting for the Violins by Justine Saracen. After surviving Dunkirk, a scarred and embittered British nurse returns to Nazi-occupied Brussels to join the Resistance, and finds that nothing is fair in love and war. (978-1-62639-046-1)

Turnbull House by Jess Faraday. London 1891: Reformed criminal Ira Adler has a new, respectable life—but will an old flame and the promise of riches tempt him back to London's dark side...and his own? (978-1-60282-987-9)

Stronger Than This by David-Matthew Barnes. A gay man and a lesbian form a beautiful friendship out of grief when their soul mates are tragically killed. (978-1-60282-988-6)

Death Came Calling by Donald Webb. When private investigator Katsuro Tanaka is hired to look into the death of a high profile lawyer, he becomes embroiled in a case of murder and mayhem. (978-1-60282-979-4)

Love in the Shadows by Dylan Madrid. While teaming up to bring a killer to justice, a lustful spark is ignited between an American man living in London and an Italian spy named Luca. (978-1-60282-981-7)

Cutie Pie Must Die by R.W. Clinger. Sexy detectives, a muscled quarterback, and the queerest murders...when murder is most cute. (978-1-60282-961-9)